Helen
Keller

From Tragedy to Triumph

Illustrated by Robert Doremus

Helen Keller

From Tragedy to Triumph

By Katharine E. Wilkie

Aladdin Paperbacks

First Aladdin Paperbacks edition 1986
Copyright © 1969 by the Bobbs-Merrill Co., Inc.

ALADDIN PAPERBACKS
An imprint of Simon & Schuster Children's Publishing Division
1230 Avenue of the Americas, New York, NY 10020

Manufactured in the United States of America
42

Library of Congress Cataloging-in-Publication Data
Wilkie, Katharine Elliot, 1904—
Helen Keller : from tragedy to triumph.
Reprint. Originally published: Indianapolis: Bobbs-Merrill, 1969.
Summary: A biography, focusing on the childhood years,
of the blind and deaf woman who overcame her handicaps
with the help of her teacher, Annie Sullivan.
1. Keller, Helen, 1880–1968—Juvenile literature.   2. Sullivan, Annie,
1866–1936—Juvenile literature.   3. Blind-deaf—United States—Biography—
Juvenile literature.   4. Teachers of blind–deaf—United States—
Juvenile literature.   [1. Keller, Helen, 1880–1968.   2. Blind-deaf.   3. Deaf.
4. Physically handicapped.]   I. Title.
HV1624.K4W52   1986   362.4'1'0924 [B] [92]   86-10719
ISBN-13: 978-0-02-041980-8 (Aladdin pbk.)
ISBN-10: 0-02-041980-5 (Aladdin pbk.)
0917 OFF

To Lydia

Illustrations

Full Pages

Numerous smaller illustrations

Contents

Books by Katharine E. Wilkie

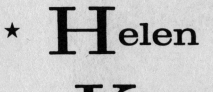

Helen Keller

From Tragedy to Triumph

Alone in
the Dark

"COME AND GET the mixing bowl!" the cook Viney called from the kitchen.

The three children were playing under a big water oak tree in the backyard at Ivy Green. The two Negro children, Martha Washington and Percy, sprang to their feet. They raced to see who could reach the kitchen door first. Five-year-old Helen Keller did not even look up. She went on rocking her rag doll Nancy.

"Be sure that Helen gets her share," Viney commanded as she handed the bowl out the kitchen door to Martha Washington. Martha took it and handed three spoons to Percy.

Martha Washington giggled. "You'd better hope she leaves a bite or two for Percy and me, Ma. You know she'll go wild when she tastes that good old cake batter."

Viney frowned. "It wouldn't matter if the poor little lamb ate it all." She looked past the children at Helen, who was sitting on the grass with her head bent over her doll.

The children took the bowl and ran back to the oak tree. Helen had not known they were gone. She could not see the pink and white hollyhocks back of her Alabama home. She could not hear the bees in the honeysuckle.

She had been very ill when she was nineteen months old. For a time the doctor had thought she would not live. Then she got well, but the illness left her blind, deaf, and dumb. Now she was a strong, healthy little girl almost six years old, but she could neither see nor hear.

Martha Washington squatted down beside

Helen. She handed a spoon to Percy, but she laid Helen's spoon on the grass. Percy's eyes shone as he reached into the mixing bowl. He filled his spoon and popped it greedily into his mouth. Then he rubbed his stomach and grinned. "Um-m-m!" he said. "It's good!"

Martha filled her spoon and raised it to her lips. Suddenly she stopped and looked toward Helen, who still held her doll.

"You'd better get your share first," Percy told his sister. He glanced fleetingly from one girl to the other. "When Helen tastes it, she'll be like a tiger with raw meat."

Martha laughed. She knew exactly what he meant. When Helen wanted anything, she acted like a little wild animal until she got it. Martha ate two spoonfuls of cake batter. Percy followed her example. When he reached for a third helping, Martha pulled his arm back.

"No!" she said. "It's Helen's turn now."

"The batter isn't half gone," Percy objected. "It's not fair for her to have so much."

Martha frowned at him. "It's not fair for her not to see or hear or talk, either." She placed her brown hand gently over Helen's hand. Helen pushed it aside and held her doll closer.

Martha reached for Helen's hand again. This time Helen slapped it away. Then Martha pushed the handle of the spoon into her hand.

Now Helen smiled. She understood what Martha was doing. With her two playmates Helen always scraped the bowl when Viney made a cake. Martha set the bowl in Helen's lap. The blind child filled her spoon and lifted it to her mouth.

She was very happy. Even if she could not see or hear, she could taste and smell and feel. She dropped the spoon on the grass and ran her finger along the inside of the bowl. Then she stuck out a little pink tongue and licked it.

14

"No manners," Percy said to Martha.

"Oh, hush," his sister returned crossly. She really agreed with Percy, but she felt sorry for their friend. She was thankful to be able to see and hear and speak.

Helen was independent and wanted no pity. She crammed her mouth full of the tasty mixture. She filled the spoon again and waved it beneath her nose. She smelled sugar, spices, and freshly churned butter. She sighed happily.

Percy pushed his spoon into the bowl again and his hand brushed against Helen's. She slapped it sharply. Then she pinched him.

"Ouch!" he cried.

Martha Washington gave a little shrug. "It serves you right," she said. "You know how she acts when anyone crosses her."

Viney stuck her head out the kitchen door. "You, Martha Washington! Percy!" she called. "What are you doing to Helen?"

"Nothing, Ma," Martha protested. "You'd better ask what she is doing to us."

"You treat my baby lamb right," commanded Viney. "Give her whatever she wants. The poor child doesn't even know how to want much."

It was a hot July morning in the little town of Tuscumbia. The captain was ready to leave for the office of the *North Alabamian*. He was editor and publisher of the small newspaper.

"Why don't you let Helen help Martha Washington and Percy in the vegetable garden?" Captain Keller asked his wife. "She can pick beans as well as they can."

Mrs. Keller shook her head. "The sun is too hot. The heat might make her sick."

"She is already sick," Captain Keller growled. He looked ashamed the moment he spoke. "I didn't mean it, Kate. She is as strong and healthy in body as any child I ever saw. But she is becoming harder to deal with every day. She acts

16

more like a child from the slums than a little southern lady. What can we do with her?"

Two big tears rolled down his wife's cheeks. The captain came near and patted her gently on the shoulder. "There, there," he told her. "You do mighty well with her. Just keep on managing her as you really think best."

Kate Keller wiped her eyes. "I have been reading Charles Dickens' *American Notes*, in which he tells about a man named Dr. Samuel Gridley Howe. This man founded a wonderful school in Boston called Perkins Institute. Do you suppose Helen could be helped there?"

"The Perkins School is mainly for blind people," Captain Keller reminded her. "Our daughter is deaf and dumb as well as blind."

"Mr. Dickens wrote in his book about a deaf, dumb, and blind child named Laura Bridgman," Mrs. Keller went on. "Dr. Howe brought her to Perkins School when she was only eight years old. She must be nearly sixty by now. Dr. Howe did great things for her, according to Mr. Dickens. He taught her the alphabet by touch. Now she reads and writes. Do you think the Perkins School might help our Helen?"

Captain Keller shook his head. "I doubt it, Kate," he said sadly. "You can't believe all you read in books."

After Captain Keller left, Mrs. Keller prepared to go to the kitchen at the back of the house. She planned to make pies for supper. Viney was busy doing the washing. Before she went to the kitchen, Mrs. Keller took a last look at baby Mildred. The baby was cooing in her cradle, ready to go to sleep.

Mrs. Keller led Helen to the kitchen. Viney had set up her laundry tubs behind the kitchen. Martha Washington and Percy were pulling weeds in the vegetable garden. Mrs. Keller and Helen were alone in the kitchen.

18

Mrs. Keller seated the little girl on the bare, scrubbed floor and gave her several shining pots and pans to play with. She decided to make cherry pies. She measured out the lard and mixed it with the flour. Then she added a little water to make dough. She rolled out the dough and placed it in the piepan.

She looked down at Helen. The child was pretending to hold something in her left hand. She picked up a make-believe object in her right hand and made spreading movements.

Mrs. Keller laughed. "Bless her! She is spreading a slice of bread with butter."

Helen soon tired of this game. Now she moved her arm in circles. Her mother laid down the rolling pin and watched her. She took an eggbeater and handed it to Helen.

The little girl threw it to the floor. She did not want the eggbeater. Her mother was puzzled. Then she understood. She got a wooden ice cream bucket from the pantry and placed it on the floor within Helen's reach.

The child gave the handle a few turns. She felt inside the bucket for the metal container. She knew it by its shape and cold, smooth surface. She went back to turning the crank, and the metal container went round and round.

Meanwhile Mrs. Keller filled two piepans with a hot cherry mixture she had been cooking on the big iron stove. She covered the tops of the pies with strips of pastry. Next she opened the oven door and placed the pies inside.

By now Helen was close beside her, holding fast to her mother's skirts. She was close to the stove, and her mother pulled her back.

"Hot!" Mrs. Keller told her little daughter. "Helen will be burned." Then she sighed. Sometimes she forgot that Helen could not hear. The child shook off her mother's hand. She did not like to be stopped by anyone.

Mrs. Keller scooped up the scraps of dough from the table. She made them into a lump and handed them to her daughter. This was something new. Helen sat down again. She liked to push the soft dough into different shapes.

Mrs. Keller took a piece of hard candy from the cupboard and dropped it into Helen's mouth. The little girl was contented. Her hands were busy and she liked the sweet taste of the candy. She sat quietly and played with the dough. Her mother stood for a moment watching her quiet contentment, but she knew that the child would not remain quiet very long.

Mrs. Keller remembered that she must check the sugar barrel. Captain Keller would buy more sugar when the supply ran low. She glanced down at Helen. She would leave her for only a few seconds. She went to the front door of the kitchen and listened, but there was no sound. Evidently the baby was asleep.

She took a key from the ring at her waistband
and fitted it into the lock on the pantry door.
Then she turned the key and swung the door
open. At that moment Helen, tiring of her play-
things, rose to her feet. She did not know her

22

mother had gone into the pantry. She felt her way along the wall of the kitchen. Presently she came to the pantry door and gave it a hard push.

"Open the door, Helen," Mrs. Keller called from inside. She had forgotten again that her daughter could not hear her.

By now Helen had found the key with her quick fingers. She knew what keys were for. She tightened her hold on this one and turned it. There was a sharp click.

"What have you done!" her mother called. She shook the door with all her might. Nothing happened. Helen was in her own dark world where there was no sound.

Mrs. Keller began to pound on the door on the other side. Somehow Helen could feel the thumping, but she did not know what it meant. She laughed aloud. This was great fun.

An hour later Viney finished her washing. She had been working hard. A long line of sheets and wearing apparel blew in the breeze. She heard Mrs. Keller's cries as she came near the kitchen. She broke into a run and burst in at the kitchen door. By now Helen was fast asleep in a corner of the room. Viney took one look at her. Then she rushed for the pantry door.

"Help! help!" cried Mrs. Keller. "I'm locked in the pantry."

"Great suffering balls of fire!" exclaimed Viney. "I'll let you out."

Viney turned the key and opened the door, and Mrs. Keller stumbled out. She had been shut in the dark little room for more than an hour and had feared that Helen was in danger. She had feared that baby Mildred might be hurt.

Viney, her kind face distressed, led her to a chair and poured her a glass of water. "It's all over now," she said. She turned and frowned at the sleeping Helen. "I've a good mind to turn that child across my knee."

24

"You will do nothing of the sort," Helen's mother declared. "You musn't lay a hand on her. She didn't know what she was doing."

Viney looked unhappy. "I know she didn't. I shouldn't have said that. I wouldn't hurt a hair of her pretty head, Miss Kate. I love that child as if she were my own."

Mrs. Keller wiped her eyes on the corner of her apron. "My poor little girl! What will become of us? What are we going to do, Viney?"

The Negro woman turned from the oven. She was taking out the pies. They were well-browned but not burned. She looked with pity at the two people in her kitchen. Helen's mother had gathered her sleeping daughter up in her loving arms.

"I guess we'll just have to trust the good Lord to bring us through our troubles," Viney answered wisely.

The Trip North

HELEN WAS very excited. She was riding on the railroad train with her father and mother. They were on their way to Baltimore, Maryland, to see a famous doctor. "Maybe Dr. Chisholm can help her," Mrs. Keller said.

"I certainly hope so, my dear," answered Captain Keller. "Our doctor says there is no better eye doctor in the country."

Helen knew nothing of what they were saying. Her blindness and deafness shut her out of their world, but she was happy because things were happening. She was going somewhere, and she was wearing her best clothes.

Both her father and mother were with her. There were times when she could not find her father. She had no way of knowing that he went to his newspaper office every day.

Helen could feel the roll of the train wheels, *dum-te-dum--dum-te-dum--dum-te-dum--dum-te-dum.* She liked their motion. She had never felt anything like it before.

The conductor in his blue uniform came down the aisle. "Your tickets, please," he said. Captain Keller handed him the tickets. The man punched them and handed them back. Helen felt the sharp clip-clip of the punch and reached out to find out what was happening.

"No, no," Mother said. She drew Helen's hands back. The conductor readily saw that Helen was blind. Then her parents told him that she was deaf and dumb, too.

"Let me take her with me," he said. "I have only a few more tickets to punch. I'll bring her back soon. She can play with the punch after that until time for lunch." He took her by the hand and led her down the aisle. The passengers turned to look at her.

"I see you have a helper," a man said with a smile. "How do you like being the conductor's helper, little girl?"

"She can't hear you," the conductor told him. "She can't see you, either."

"How dreadful!" the man replied.

"This box is full of shells I picked up at the seashore," a woman said. "Let the poor child have them. Perhaps she will enjoy playing with them." The woman handed the conductor a cardboard box, which was tied with string.

Other passengers who had overheard the conductor's words shook their heads as they looked at Helen. They were sorry for her.

All the while Helen was smiling. She liked the firm touch of the conductor's hand. She liked

28

the feel of the clip-clip every time he let her punch a ticket. She liked the roll of the wheels beneath her feet.

After a while the conductor brought her back to her seat. "She was my little helper," he told her parents. "She made several friends, too, and a lady gave her this box of seashells." He handed the box to Helen's mother. Then he helped the little girl up on the seat and handed her the punch. "I don't need it now," he said. "She may play with it until I come back."

Mr. Keller found a piece of cardboard and handed it to Helen. She knew exactly what to do with it. She pressed the punch eagerly. *Clip-clip! Clip-clip!* went the punch. *Dum-te-dum! Dum-te-dum!* went the train wheels.

Helen was busy and contented. She punched holes in the cardboard. Little white dots fell in her lap. They fell on the seat. They fell all over the floor. Helen was happy.

"You are making a mess," said Mother. "I'm ashamed of you."

The conductor, who was passing by, overheard her. "Don't worry, ma'am," he said. "The porter will be glad to clean up after her. He has a little girl of his own at home."

While Helen was playing with the punch, her father made a small hole in each of the shells. When the conductor needed the punch again, Mr. Keller gave Helen the shells. She traced the ridges and curves of the delicate shells with her sensitive fingers. Then her father showed her how to string the shells together with the string which had been tied around the box.

At last the Kellers arrived in Baltimore. "People have been kind and Helen has enjoyed every minute of the trip," said her mother in amazement. "We had expected that she would find the trip long and tiresome, but she has been a good traveler all the way here."

The Kellers took a carriage from the train station to the hotel. Helen liked riding in the carriage as well as she liked riding in a train. *Clop-clop-clop* went the horse's hoofs as the carriage rolled along. There were other carriages on the street. There were also delivery vans and men and boys on bicycles.

There were hundreds of tall buildings. Many of them were still being built. People were hurrying to and fro. Helen could not see the diverse activities of this great city and she could not hear the various sounds. Yet somehow she could sense the bustling and the noise.

The next day the Kellers went to see Dr. Chisholm. Their family doctor had written to tell him they were coming. Dr. Chisholm had many strange-looking instruments in his office with which to test people. He used some of them to perform tests on Helen. He tested her ears and her eyes in several different ways.

At last he shook his head. "I can do nothing for her," he said. "Her early illness has destroyed her sight and hearing completely."

He patted Helen on the head. He was a kind man, and he knew that her parents were broken-hearted. "Have you ever heard of Dr. Alexander Graham Bell?" he asked them. "He has done some fine work with deaf persons. I suggest that you go to Washington and see him."

The Kellers wasted no time in following Dr. Chisholm's advice. A short time later, on a hot summer afternoon, they took Helen to Dr. Bell's office in Washington.

Dr. Bell was a tall, broad-shouldered, handsome man with dark bushy whiskers and bright, sparkling eyes. He took Helen on his knee and she made friends with him at once. He held his fine gold watch up to her ear. The watch not only ticked away the seconds and told the minutes, but it struck the hours.

One-two-three-four. Helen could not hear the dainty musical chime, but she could feel it. She reached out her hand for the watch. Dr. Bell smiled. "No, lassie," he said.

He snapped the case shut and put it in his pocket. Helen's father and mother waited anxiously, wondering how she would act when the doctor didn't give her the watch. To their surprise, she seemed to be contented. Dr. Bell stroked her golden hair lightly. She sensed his sympathy and was happy because he understood her signs.

"He certainly has a way with her," Mrs. Keller whispered to her husband.

Dr. Bell heard her. His eyes twinkled. "I have learned, madam. I have learned. My wife and my mother are both deaf."

"But not blind," Mr. Keller added sadly.

"No, not blind," Dr. Bell said. "This little lady has a double share of trouble." He continued to stroke Helen's hair while he looked thoughtfully at the sad-faced parents. He had promised them nothing, yet they felt hopeful after they had been with him this short time.

At last he spoke. "It may be possible to help her. Have you ever heard of the Perkins School for the Blind in Boston?"

"I have read about it in Mr. Dickens' *American Notes*," said Mrs. Keller eagerly. "It was begun by Dr. Samuel Gridley Howe."

"The world lost a very great man when Sam Howe died," explained Dr. Bell. "The school is now run by his son-in-law, Michael Anagnos from Greece. Why don't you write to Mr. Anagnos and ask him to send you a special teacher to work with Helen?"

Little Savage

Six-year-old helen stood on the front porch at Ivy Green. Everyone was hurrying about. She could feel them brush against her as they went by, but no one seemed to have any time for her. Once Mrs. Keller stopped and kissed her little daughter on the forehead.

Helen held fast to her. She loved the cool soft touch of her mother's lips and tightened her hands on her mother's dress.

Mrs. Keller gently removed the child's sticky fingers and hurried away. She wanted everything to be ready for Miss Anne Sullivan, the teacher from Perkins School in Boston.

"That child is a sight!" exclaimed Captain Keller. "Aren't you going to clean her up?"

"I put fresh clothes on her less than an hour ago," Mrs. Keller told him unhappily. "She got away from Martha Washington, who was supposed to be watching her. Then she found a pitcher of grape juice on the kitchen table. If you think she is a sight, look at the kitchen."

Viney spoke from the doorway. "Let me try to dress her again, Miss Kate."

Mrs. Keller shook her head. "There won't be time to dress her again. We'll have to let her stay as she is. The carriage should be returning at any moment now. I heard the train whistle at least fifteen minutes ago."

Martha Washington and Percy had gone down to the entrance at the road to watch for the carriage. Now they came flying across the meadow and up the front walk. "She's coming!" they screamed on the way to the house.

They ran like deer past Helen. Somehow she felt the motion. She reached out her hands to catch them, but she felt only empty air.

The carriage turned into the avenue between the two stone pillars. It rolled slowly toward the house and stopped before the small gate in the front yard. The Negro driver climbed down to open the door for his passenger.

Father and Mother hurried down the steps to greet the new arrival. Viney in a white starched apron waited just inside the house. For once Martha Washington and Percy were a little shy. They waited with her. Helen was left alone on the front porch. She sensed that something was going on, but she did not know what it was.

The traveler, a shabbily-dressed young Irish-woman barely out of her teens, stepped down from the carriage. Her clothes, which were too heavy for the mild southern weather, were mussed and wrinkled from the long journey.

She was smiling, but the firm set of her chin made her look as though she meant business. Although she was aware of her unfashionable appearance, she held her head high. She was glad that dark glasses hid her red, aching eyes from everyone. She did not want anyone to find out how lonely and bewildered she felt. This was the farthest she had ever been from Perkins School in Boston, Massachusetts.

The captain held out his hand. "I am Captain Keller, Miss Sullivan," he said. "This is my wife and yonder is Helen."

Anne Sullivan shook hands with the Kellers and raised her dark glasses to look at Helen. The child had never looked worse. Her hair was tangled and unbrushed. Her dress was soiled and torn. She looked cross. No one had stopped to humor her the whole day.

Miss Sullivan had expected her pupil to be frail and sickly. She was surprised to see that

Helen had rosy cheeks and looked strong and healthy. Also she noted that Helen was somewhat larger than other children of the same age with whom she had worked at Perkins School.

Almost at once the young teacher was attracted to Helen and became eager to work with her. She felt that the child was attractive, even though she was blind and more or less expressionless. She longed to make her smile and to bring out some of her attractive features.

Miss Sullivan walked across the grass and up the steps. She took a long look at Helen. The Kellers, along with Viney and the two children, silently watched her and waited. Then she bent over and kissed Helen lightly on the cheek.

The child sensed that this was not her mother. Here was a stranger. She instantly became a little wild animal. She promptly shoved with all her strength at the newcomer.

The teacher was not expecting this reaction.

She was caught off guard but soon recovered her composure. She set her hat more firmly on her head and stood there.

Helen rushed at Miss Sullivan again, but the young teacher was ready and caught her in her arms. The child beat wildly and fiercely with her fists to get away. Finally the teacher seized her hands and held them fast.

"Now see here--" Captain Keller began.

Mrs. Keller hurried forward and put a bit of candy into Helen's mouth. The little girl liked the taste. Slowly she stopped struggling and her arms dropped to her sides. She sank down on the steps and smacked her lips noisily.

"Just as you would give a bone to a dog," said Miss Sullivan hotly. Captain Keller watched and wondered what would happen next.

Suddenly Helen stood up and pulled Miss Sullivan's face down to hers. The young teacher sat down on the step beside her. Now she was on a level with the child. She watched the little girl's expression and movements with interest.

Helen ran her fingers over each part of Miss Sullivan's face. She carefully explored all the details. She traced the wide, full mouth. She felt the high cheek bones and the well-shaped chin. She felt the dark hair drawn back from the smooth forehead. All the while she seemed to be curious and uncertain.

Then suddenly with searching fingers she found the dark glasses that covered Miss Sullivan's eyes. Her busy fingers stopped and she looked up inquiringly. All at once Miss Sullivan started to talk. "I've been blind, too," she said. "I've had nine operations. Even now I don't see very well, and the light hurts my eyes."

"She can't understand a word you say," Mrs. Keller reminded her.

"Neither can a baby," Miss Sullivan replied. "Yet we talk to babies." She turned her dark glasses on Mrs. Keller. "Someday she will understand me. Now may I go up to my room? I should like to tidy up a bit before supper. I'd like to take Helen with me."

Captain and Mrs. Keller stood openmouthed. Most visitors didn't have the patience to try to win Helen's attention or affection. This young lady from Boston seemed not only to welcome the touch of the child's fingers but really to want Helen with her. Viney and the children seemed as surprised as the Kellers.

Miss Sullivan took one of Helen's grimy hands in hers and pointed it upward. Helen jerked her hand away. The teacher took her hand again and again she jerked it away. Patiently the young woman reached for her hand a third time, hoping the child would understand.

At last Helen nodded her head. She understood what the girl from Boston wanted. She stood up and tugged at Miss Sullivan's hand.

The young teacher reached for her worn leather bag. She held her head high. She had won the first round with her pupil. "I think Helen will come with me," she said with a smile.

Mrs. Keller recovered her voice. "Viney, please show Miss Sullivan to her room."

The captain stepped forward. "Allow me to carry your bag, Miss Sullivan."

Miss Sullivan clutched the bag with both hands. "I want Helen to know that it belongs to me," she said. "I'll carry it myself." Then she marched firmly up the stairs behind Viney, who led the way. Helen stumbled along behind them.

The four people in the lower hall stared up the stairs. "I don't understand her," the captain exclaimed. "She doesn't have good manners, and she is entirely too young. I'm afraid we have made a mistake in getting her."

Mrs. Keller sat staring straight ahead and was slow to answer. "I think I am going to like her," she said slowly. "Captain, this may be the greatest day of our lives."

Nine-year-old Martha Washington and her brother Percy watched and wondered. "Just you wait," whispered Martha. "Before long Helen will decide to play a trick on the lady."

Upstairs in the bedroom Helen sat in the middle of the floor, holding Miss Sullivan's watch to her ear. She could not hear its ticking, but she could feel the movement.

Miss Sullivan moved about the room. She hung her few dresses in the closet and placed other articles in the drawers of the dresser. She was eager to get her things put away so she could give attention to the child.

At last she sat down in a chair and watched Helen closely. By now the child was off in her own private world, the world she knew best. She knew people only through taste, smell, or touch. Seeing and hearing meant nothing to her.

The child scrambled to her feet. She was be-coming restless. She turned this way and that. She put out her hands to feel her way about.

Soon a servant brought Miss Sullivan's trunk up from the carriage house. Helen knew that something was happening and started to explore. She wandered about the room and finally dis-covered the trunk, which was something new and different in the house.

She passed her hands quickly over the trunk and seemed almost to try to see it with her hands. She felt for the keyhole. Miss Sullivan opened her purse and took out the key to the trunk. She handed the key to Helen.

The little girl seized the key eagerly. She thrust it into the keyhole and turned it. Then she swung the lid open. "You are very clever," observed Miss Sullivan.

Helen dug into the trunk and pulled out a rusty black shawl. She draped it about her shoulders. "That shawl looks no better on you than on me," thought Miss Sullivan. "After all I didn't come here dressed in the latest Paris fashions, but I have a roof over my head and a salary of twenty-five dollars a month. That isn't too bad for a girl with no family to turn to."

By now Helen was down on her knees in front of the trunk. She was throwing its contents right and left. The shawl had slipped to the floor. She had forgotten all about it.

In her search she was making meaningless little noises, which seemed more like those of an animal than a child. Soon she came upon a box of hard candies and took off the lid. She dug into the sweets with both hands.

Miss Sullivan sprang to her feet. "No, no! You cannot eat that way," she said.

She pulled the box away from Helen, and the child fought to keep it. Helen kicked and struggled and candy flew from one end of the room

to the other. Miss Sullivan did not give up, but started to pick up the candy.

There was a battle royal. As a small child, Miss Sullivan had lived in a very poor neighborhood. She had learned to fight for her rights and naturally found herself fighting again, but this time with a child.

She dragged Helen into the hall and seated her on a bench. Then she returned to her bedroom, slammed the door behind her, and sank into the nearest chair. By now she felt greatly exhausted. "Whew!" she panted. "I'd almost as soon fight a tornado as that child."

There was no doubt that Helen was outside. She began to beat on the wall with her fists and to stamp on the floor with her feet. Also she gave off sounds from her voiceless throat like those of a wild beast.

"You are a badly spoiled young lady as well as a clever one," Miss Sullivan said aloud. "This is a poor way to begin my teaching, but what else can I do? I have a feeling that we shall do battle many times in the future."

She smoothed her hair and bathed her face for relief. She put drops from a small medicine bottle into her eyes. Then she looked down at her belongings cluttered about the floor and started slowly to put them away.

The sounds outside had changed. By now Helen seemed to be beating her head against the wall. "Go ahead and beat some sense into that stubborn head of yours, young lady," said Miss Sullivan, "but remember that I am as stubborn as you are. It seems evident that I must not only teach you, but I must tame you, too."

After a time the noise stopped. Miss Sullivan went on putting things away. In a few minutes she would open the door. By then she hoped for a truce between her and her pupil.

In the hall Helen had risen to her feet. She

felt her way along the wall to the bedroom door. She ran her hands over its flat surface until she found the lock with the key still in place. Then she did the only thing that she knew how to do with the key. She turned it in the lock and there was a little click.

Inside the bedroom Miss Sullivan heard the sound. She knew at once what had happened. She forgot that Helen could not hear her. "Let me out!" she cried. "Let me out!"

Helen could only feel the shaking door. She did not know what it meant. The Kellers were out in the yard. Viney and her children were in their cabin. Miss Sullivan was locked in.

The Little House in the Garden

HELEN, who rarely sat down properly for her meals, was wandering around the breakfast table. Miss Sullivan looked on with disapproval as she roamed like a puppy from person to person. Her father popped a piece of crisp bacon into her mouth. She swallowed it and moved on to her mother, who gave her a spoonful of egg.

"I hope Helen's little prank last night didn't upset you," said Captain Keller.

Miss Sullivan looked up and her mouth became firmer. "I don't upset easily," she replied, "but I would hardly call Helen's act of locking me in my room a simple prank."

The captain looked surprised. "She did the same thing to her mother not many months ago," he said. "Of course, you understand that she didn't know what she was doing."

"I do understand, sir," replied Miss Sullivan, "and she must be taught to understand, too. She might do something dangerous to someone."

"Have you any suggestions?" the captain asked her coldly. He was not accustomed to having his ideas questioned. He was beginning to think that he did not care for this plain-spoken young woman from Boston.

By now Helen had arrived at Miss Sullivan's plate. Her quick little fingers darted out and snatched a handful of scrambled eggs. Miss Sullivan seized her wrists. "No! No!"

"She can't hear you!" cried the captain.

Helen gave a howl of anger and threw the handful of eggs to the floor, spattering both Miss Sullivan's dress and chair. Then she hit back at Miss Sullivan as hard as she could. The young woman's Irish temper flared. She rapped Helen sharply on a wrist.

The child reached for the plate once more and succeeded in getting a handful of eggs. She started to reach the third time, but this was too much for Miss Sullivan. She pushed the plate beyond Helen's reach. Then she seized the offender by the shoulders and shook her for a moment as hard as she could.

Captain Keller rose abruptly to his feet and gave an angry snort. "Miss Sullivan!" he cried. "No one has ever dared to lay a finger on my poor unfortunate child."

Miss Sullivan's hands were still on Helen's shoulders as she turned to face the master of Ivy Green. "Then it's high time someone did. She is the worst spoiled child I have ever seen. She actually is a little savage."

By now Helen had thrown herself to the floor.

Her heels were drumming up and down on the floor, raising a cloud of dust on the carpet. Tears were streaming from her eyes. She rubbed them until her face was streaked and dirty.

Mrs. Keller stooped over to pick her up. The screaming child struck her in the face. "It's Mother, baby!" the poor woman exclaimed. "I'm only trying to help you."

Captain Keller ran his fingers through his hair and paced the floor. Martha Washington and Percy looked into the room from a safe distance. "I've never seen Helen carrying on this bad," Martha whispered to Percy.

Percy giggled. "The new lady had better take care. When Helen's tiger temper gets loose, she will claw anybody that gets in her way."

Twenty-year-old Anne Sullivan was the only person in the room who acted calm. With her hands on her hips she stared down at the screaming child. She did not look excited.

"Now see what you have done!" Captain Keller told her angrily.

Miss Sullivan turned to face him, holding her clear-cut stubborn chin high. Her heart was beating wildly, but she did not intend for him to know it. "I treated her like a human being," she explained. "Every human being must learn sooner or later to obey rules."

"For the love of heaven, woman!" the captain shouted. "Don't you realize that the girl is not a real human being?"

Miss Sullivan gave him a long look. "She is a real human being, and she deserves to be treated like one. Any other treatment is cruel."

"There is just one way to deal with her," he said. "Give her everything she wants. We have known that for several years."

"Sometimes it isn't good for a child to have everything she wants," Miss Sullivan replied in a cool, firm tone of voice.

"But Helen isn't a normal child," Mrs. Keller reminded her.

"Perhaps she is more normal than you think, if you will only give her a chance."

The captain spoke above the noise of Helen's screeching. "We hired you to teach Helen, not to tell us how to deal with her. We did not hire you to run our family. Unless you change your ways, you'll have to leave."

Miss Sullivan's heart sank. She wondered whether she could go back to Perkins School. Already the authorities had kept her longer than they had kept most students.

There was no trace of fear in her face. She answered the captain firmly. "You wrote to Perkins School for a teacher. I cannot teach Helen until I can control her."

She looked very small and young as she stood in front of the big man, but she faced him like a Spartan. By now Viney had carried Helen off to the kitchen. Through the open door Miss Sullivan could see her wiping the child's tear-stained face with a damp cloth. She was holding her and giving her something to eat.

"Viney has more sense than any of us," growled the captain. "That's the only way to handle her. Now she's calm and quiet."

Miss Sullivan shook her head. "She will only throw a temper fit the next time she doesn't get her way. You are storing up trouble, sir."

Captain Keller glared at her. "What do you propose, Miss Sullivan?"

The girl looked past the middle-aged man to his sad-faced wife. Then she looked past both of them to Helen. At last she spoke. "Your daughter has a bright, inquiring mind, but unless she can be taught to listen and to talk, her mind will remain a prisoner as long as she lives. I believe I can help her."

"You said talk!" Mrs. Keller exclaimed.

Miss Sullivan nodded . She began to move her fingers swiftly as the others watched. "There is more than one way to talk," she said. "I have just spelled H-e-l-e-n for you."

Mrs. Keller's eyes were filled with wonder. "So that is how the deaf and dumb alphabet works," she said. "I have heard about it, but I have never seen anyone use it."

"They call it the manual alphabet," Miss Sullivan quietly explained. "It was invented by Spanish monks under a vow of silence."

"But Helen can't learn it because she can't see," objected Captain Keller.

Miss Sullivan raised her chin a full inch. "Yes, but she can feel, which is her way of seeing. She will feel the letters as I spell them into her hand. I know my task will not be easy. I must have her to myself with no one else around. She is a very spoiled little girl. She must be taught to obey before she will begin to learn. Is there a place away from the family where I can take her for a time?"

Helen's father and mother looked at each other. They knew Helen was spoiled. Every-

one had been sorry for her and had spoiled her since her dreadful illness when she was only nineteen months old. They had not known what else to do under the circumstances.

Captain Keller cleared his throat. "Have you ever taught a blind and deaf child, Miss Sullivan? Frankly, we expected someone older."

The young teacher caught her breath. "I have never taught for pay before, but I have helped to teach the children at Perkins School," she replied. "A few of the children there are both blind and deaf. Every teacher in the world has to begin somewhere."

Mrs. Keller looked approvingly at Miss Sullivan and turned to her husband. "There's our little house in the garden which we use only for guests during the hunting season," she suggested. "We could get that house ready for Miss Sullivan and Helen in a few hours."

Captain Keller did not answer at once but

he seemed to be thinking. Finally he spoke. Miss Sullivan thought there might be a ghost of a twinkle in his eye. "You don't know what you are getting into," he warned her, "but I am willing for you to try it. You may move into the garden house with Helen for two weeks. Then we'll decide what to do next."

He walked out the back door and across the brick walk to the kitchen. Helen had fallen asleep in Viney's lap. His eyes grew tender as he looked at his sleeping child.

"Viney, sweep and clean the little house for Miss Sullivan and Helen," he told the Negro woman. "Take their meals to them for two weeks. Set up a cot for Percy in the small room at the rear. He will act as messenger."

Under his breath he added, "She will probably need a whole fleet of messengers."

Two Weeks Alone

"HERE THEY COME!" Martha Washington shouted at the top of her voice. Again she and Percy were perched on the top of the stone pillars at the entrance to Ivy Green. Once more they were watching for the Keller carriage.

Helen had gone for a ride with her father and mother. Meanwhile Viney had prepared the little house in the garden for Helen and her teacher. Now it was fresh and clean. White curtains hung at the windows. There was a rag rug on the floor. The table was set for two.

The little house seemed to say, "Come in! Come in! You are welcome."

Anne Sullivan hoped that Helen would think she was in a strange place. That was why Captain and Mrs. Keller had taken her for a ride. They did not feel she would recognize the little house. They had promised to leave her alone with Miss Sullivan for two whole weeks.

Viney watched the approaching carriage. She did not approve of what was going on. "Why are they pestering my poor baby lamb?" she muttered. "Why can't they leave her alone?"

The carriage rolled to a stop at the gate. Captain Keller lifted Helen to the ground. She could not see Martha Washington and Percy on the porch. She could not hear them talking.

Martha was curious and Percy felt important, holding a roll of nightclothes under his arm. For two weeks he was to be a messenger.

Percy laughed long and loudly. "The Yankee lady may have to call out the whole United States Army," he said to Martha.

Anne Sullivan, who had been waiting, stepped forward. She took Helen by the hand, but the child pulled away. Tears rolled down Mrs. Keller's cheeks. Again the teacher reached for Helen's hand. Helen's face flushed with anger, and she stamped her feet furiously.

Miss Sullivan wasted no more time. She picked up Helen, who kicked and fought. She struggled up the steps with the child, marched into the house, and closed the door.

Mrs. Keller moaned. "I can't stand it. I can't go through with it," she exclaimed.

"It's only for two weeks," her husband told her. "I promise you. I won't allow them to stay there a day more than two weeks."

He took his weeping wife by the arm and led her toward Ivy Green. Helen and her teacher were alone in the little house.

Helen's temper finally began to give way. She was becoming weak from screaming and kicking in order to have her way. After a time she rose to her feet and felt her way about the room. She hunted for the door, found it, and fingered the keyhole. Then she looked disappointed. What she had expected was not there. Miss Sullivan had locked the door and removed the key.

"So you know how locks work," said Miss Sullivan. "That little mind of yours is very busy. I wish I knew what you are thinking."

The child sat down in a rocking chair. Miss Sullivan handed her a box of seashells of various sizes and shapes. Helen felt each one carefully. Here was something new and pleasing.

"You have plenty of curiosity!" said the teacher. "You want to learn. That's good."

The evening passed slowly. At last Miss Sullivan handed Helen a nightgown . The child knew what that meant. She undressed quietly, but left her clothes in a heap on the floor. Then she climbed into the big double bed.

Miss Sullivan was ready for bed, too. She undressed and slipped in beside Helen, but the child sprang out the other side. The teacher followed her and struggled for two hours, trying to get her back into bed. All the while she felt far more like a prize fighter than a teacher. She did not know that a six-year-old could be so strong or stubborn.

At last Helen lay still on the far side of the bed. She did not move when Miss Sullivan lay down beside her. They dropped off to sleep and slept the rest of the night.

In the morning Captain Keller rapped at the door and talked with Miss Sullivan. "I thought I'd bring your breakfast as I went to the office," he said. "Besides I wanted to hear what sort of a night you had."

"It was rugged, but it ended well," Miss Sullivan explained. She carefully refrained from telling him about her struggles with Helen.

The captain peeked into the room through the open door. He particularly wanted to catch a glimpse of his small daughter. By now she was sitting on the floor in her nightgown. Close beside her was the heap of clothes which she had left on the floor the night before. There she sat looking cross and sulky.

The captain raised his eyebrows. "The morning hasn't begun very well," he said.

"We will manage," said Miss Sullivan. "Don't worry about her. Above all, she must not know that you are here."

Captain Keller had faced the enemy in battle many times. Today he walked meekly away from the little house, wondering whether or not he could face this challenge in his life.

Presently Miss Sullivan sat down at the table to eat her breakfast, leaving Helen on the floor. She was glad she could eat alone in peace and let the child wait a few minutes.

Helen's keen nose soon smelled the hot hominy grits. She made her way uncertainly across the room toward the table. Miss Sullivan hastily swallowed a sip of coffee and carried the child back. She put her down beside her clothes and placed her clothes in her hands. "No clothes, no breakfast," she said.

A struggle followed, but much less severe than the one the evening before. In a few minutes Helen gave up and dressed quietly.

"Good girl," Miss Sullivan exclaimed.

She led Helen toward the table, helped her to find a chair, and gave her an approving pat. She wanted the child to feel that she had earned her breakfast by obeying. Helen ate greedily and spilled food all around her.

"I'll teach her one thing at a time," thought Miss Sullivan. "First of all I must break through the dreadful wall of silence that separates her from the world."

When breakfast was over, Miss Sullivan went over to a chest of drawers and took out a new doll. The blind children at Perkins School had sent the doll to Miss Sullivan for Helen. She handed it to Helen and watched her discover it with her fingers. Then she took it away.

At once she began to make letters from the manual alphabet with her fingers for Helen. All the time she held the little girl's hand over her own. "D-o-l-l," she spelled.

She took Helen's fingers and shaped them to spell the same word in sign language, "D-o-l-l." Her pupil liked this new game. She seized Miss Sullivan's fingers and began to spell, "D-o-l-l."

"You are a smart girl," Miss Sullivan exclaimed. "You learn quickly."

She handed the doll to Helen. "This doll is from Perkins School," she said.

Helen seized the doll, eager to hold it and play with it again. She hugged and kissed it tenderly. She rocked it in her arms. Then once more the teacher took the doll away and spelled d-o-l-l into her hand.

Helen joined in the game. She spelled d-o-l-l once more. This went on for several minutes. At last Miss Sullivan decided to stop the game. "This time you may keep the doll," she said. "You deserve to be rewarded, only I hope you won't forget what you have learned."

The two weeks passed. Sometimes the hours went fast and sometimes they dragged. Helen learned new words every day. She learned m-u-g for mug and m-i-l-k for milk but didn't understand the difference. When her teacher gave her a mug, she spelled m-i-l-k, and when she allowed her to pour milk from a pitcher, she spelled m-u-g.

"The words are only a game to her," said Miss Sullivan wearily to herself. "She doesn't know what they mean. She doesn't realize that everything and everybody in the world has a name. How can I teach her? I must think of a way in which to reach her."

Every day Captain and Mrs. Keller looked in at the big bay window, but Helen never knew that they were there. They looked in, wondering whether the two weeks in the little house with Miss Sullivan would be worthwhile.

As the days passed, they began to see signs of improvement . Once Helen was busy crocheting a long red wool chain, and again, stringing beads. At another time she was eating supper from a plate with her napkin neatly tucked under her chin. There were no signs of the little savage she had been a short time ago.

At the end of the two weeks Miss Sullivan was not satisfied. She knew she had only begun to tame Helen. She had not taught her. As she had expected, Captain Keller came to the little house early in the morning to get the child.

"The time is up," said Captain Keller.

Miss Sullivan looked unhappy. "Yes, and I need much more time. I am sorry."

"A bargain is a bargain," said the captain.

He had brought his old setter Belle with him. Helen had discovered the dog and was playing with her. Now they were in a corner and the captain looked in their direction. "What in the world is she doing to that dog?" he asked.

Miss Sullivan looked and started to laugh. "She is teaching Belle to spell."

A smile came over the captain's face. "Does she know what she is doing?"

Miss Sullivan shook her head. "I'm afraid not."

The captain stood up. "You have worked wonders with her in these two weeks. She is a different child. We can live with her now."

"Can't you leave her here a little longer?" Miss Sullivan pleaded. "We have only begun."

Helen's father shook his head. "We miss her

73

too much, her mother and I. Besides she probably can keep on learning back in her own home with you to help her. We are grateful to you, more grateful than I can tell you."

Anne Sullivan sighed. She wished she could keep her pupil alone a week or so longer, but she knew there was no use arguing with the captain. She led Helen over to the washbowl. "Now let's make you fresh and pretty for your mother," she said calmly. "You are going home."

Helen thrust her hands into the water. She pulled them out, pointed, and patted Miss Sullivan's hand. "She wants to know the name for water," Miss Sullivan explained to the captain, "but she'll soon forget how to spell it. She must practice and practice in order to learn."

Miss Sullivan shaped her fingers to spell w-a-t-e-r. Helen felt her teacher's fingers as she was spelling. Then suddenly the teacher whirled about, as if she had made a discovery.

"What is it?" asked Captain Keller.

Silently Miss Sullivan seized Helen by the hand and led her out the door into the yard. The child went willingly, as if expecting something to happen. The captain followed. "What in the world is that teacher doing?" he thought.

Miss Sullivan led Helen to the pump in the back yard and handed her a mug. Then she placed her hand with the mug under the spout of the pump. She pushed the handle up and down, causing cold water to pour out into and over the mug. Some of it fell on Helen's outstretched hand. She liked the feeling.

There was not a moment to lose. Miss Sullivan placed Helen's other hand lightly over her own. Rapidly she spelled w-a-t-e-r. Again she pumped cold water from the well, causing it to pour over Helen's hand. Once more she spelled w-a-t-er for the child.

A sudden light dawned on Helen's face. She

75

seized the pump handle from Miss Sullivan. This time she herself pumped the water from deep in the ground. When it fell on her hands, she moved her fingers with purpose. "W-a-t-e-r," she spelled. "W-a-t-e-r," she spelled again.

The teacher's face was as happy as the child's. "Helen understands!" she cried. "Before she has only copied me, but now she understands."

Helen was quivering with eagerness. She touched the pump and tugged hard at Miss Sullivan's hand. "P-u-m-p," spelled the teacher.

Three laughing persons made their way to the big house. They did not go very fast because Helen stopped a dozen times on the way to learn the names of familiar things. Before this moment she had known them only by how they felt.

Miss Sullivan spelled many words. G-r-o-u-n-d. V-i-n-e. T-r-e-l-l-i-s. W-i-n-d-o-w. T-r-e-e. B-u-s-h. When they passed Viney carrying little Mildred, Helen learned b-a-b-y.

When they reached Ivy Green, Captain Keller made a courtly bow at the door. "Miss Sullivan, you have performed a miracle," he said.

Miss Sullivan did not have time to answer. Helen was pulling at her hand. She threw her arms around the teacher. "Now she even wants to know my name!" exclaimed Miss Sullivan.

"Well, tell her," urged the captain.

Miss Sullivan hesitated. Then she spelled t-e-a-c-h-e-r. Helen rushed into her open arms. Their friendship had begun. The education of Helen Keller was well under way.

The Circus

From this time on Ivy Green seemed like a different place. Mrs. Keller was happy as she supervised the activities of the household. Captain Keller was so pleased with the surroundings that he disliked to leave the house for the newspaper office each morning. He wished he could spend all his time at home.

Helen followed Miss Sullivan everywhere outdoors on the big farm. She felt the newly plowed ground and learned to spell g-r-o-u-n-d. She made friends with the horses, mules, turkeys, chickens, dogs, and cats and spelled all their names. At the same time she learned many things about the interesting ways in which these animals lived and were cared for on the farm.

The climax for Mr. Keller came when Helen learned to spell p-a-p-a with her fingers. Every afternoon after work the captain came in the front gate and called, "Where's my little woman?" Then Helen, assisted by her teacher, would run to meet him, her arms outstretched.

One day Miss Sullivan drew the captain aside to talk for a few minutes. She asked whether she could take Helen to a circus. At first Mr. Keller objected, but at last he consented. The teacher turned to Helen and spelled, "You and I are going to the circus."

"Circus?" Helen spelled back. "What's a circus?" She was always eager to learn.

The teacher hesitated a moment. "You'll see elephants, lions, tigers, horses, and monkeys," she spelled out. "You'll see clowns, tight-rope walkers, and trapeze artists."

Helen looked happily bewildered. If Miss Sullivan wanted her to go to the circus, she knew that she would enjoy it.

By now Helen was beginning to read raised letters. Miss Sullivan helped her to read many interesting stories about wild animals. Then she pricked out additional sentences of her own for her pupil's eager fingers.

Helen soon came to know about many animals far away, but she had never "seen" them with her fingers. She could hardly wait for Miss Sullivan to show her elephants, zebras, lions, tigers, and all the others.

The morning of the circus dawned bright and clear, and Helen was even ready to skip breakfast. She was eager to leave so that she would have time to "see" everything at the circus. Her busy little fingers spelled out questions faster than the grownups could answer them.

At last Helen and the teacher started off.

Everyone in the little town of Tuscumbia seemed to be going to the circus and everybody was happy. The thrilling music of the steam calliope could be heard in the distance.

Some persons in the crowd looked at Miss Sullivan and Helen. They could not understand why a teacher would bring a little blind girl to the circus. "She can't see," they said. "Why bring her here?" All the while Anne Sullivan knew better. She knew that Helen could "see" better than many persons who had eyes.

Helen sniffed the air. "What do I smell?"

"That is the circus smell," Miss Sullivan told her. "You smell animals and sawdust."

Helen sniffed again. "I smell buttered popcorn, too. And I smell hot dogs broiling. Let's stop and buy something to eat."

"We will later," the teacher promised. "First let's look at the animals."

They stopped to see the monkeys. The small

animals were scrambling up and down the inside of their wire cage. Miss Sullivan walked up to the keeper of the monkeys in the cage. "This little girl is blind and deaf," she said. "Will you let her hold a monkey?"

The man hesitated. He looked down at Helen. "Won't she be afraid?"

Miss Sullivan's mouth turned up at the corners. "I haven't found anything yet that she is afraid of. She won't be afraid of a monkey."

In a moment Helen felt a tiny creature on her shoulder. She reached up to touch the little animal. It had hands and a wee wrinkled face. It had a long tail that ended in a circle.

Helen clapped her hands with glee. The monkey snatched at her hair ribbon. By this time the keeper had taken another monkey from the cage. This monkey playfully grabbed Helen's hat from her head and placed it on his head. The bystanders roared with laughter.

The monkeys were only the beginning. Helen and the teacher stopped at the giraffe's pen. The keeper lifted Helen up, up, up! She felt the strange animal's long neck. There was nothing like this on the farm.

Next they came to the bears' cage. A big black bear put a shaggy paw between the iron bars. "Shake hands with him," said the keeper. "He won't hurt you. He's tame."

A short time later Miss Sullivan placed three peanuts in Helen's open palm and said, "Now hold out your hand." Helen obeyed but jumped when she felt something moist touch her hand. She was elated to find that an elephant was reaching out his trunk to get the peanuts.

A little farther on, Helen shook hands with the Oriental Princess. "This is the princess who rides the elephant in the parade and in the ring," explained Miss Sullivan.

The princess was elaborately dressed. Her

costume contained spangles of green and gold and her headdress contained green and gold jewels. She even wore green and gold bracelets on her arms. "How would the little girl like to ride with me on the elephant?" she asked.

"She would love to!" Miss Sullivan replied. "She loves to do everything."

During the show Helen rode high up on the elephant in front of the Oriental Princess. She could feel the big animal's steps as he lumbered around the ring. She smiled happily, and the people in the audience cheered. They were glad to see the little girl having so much fun riding with the princess.

There was one last treat in store for Helen. She wanted to touch a lion, but the lion trainer shook his head. "No one but me ever goes into the cage with these dangerous fellows," he said. "I've been working with them for years, and I still can't tell what they will do."

The teacher spelled his words to Helen. The little girl looked disappointed. Miss Sullivan had told her many stories about lions.

Suddenly the trainer said, "Wait a minute. Maybe I can let her touch a lion after all." He disappeared behind some curtains and soon came back carrying a furry lion cub. He laid the baby lion in Helen's arms.

The child held her cheek to the thick, tawny fur. She stroked the young animal lovingly. The lion cub liked these strokes and made odd noises in his throat. Helen could feel them with her hands. "He's purring!" she cried.

Miss Sullivan sighed and thought back to her own childhood, which had not been very happy. Helen sensed that the teacher had sighed and pulled her face down to hers. Then she touched her fingers to the teacher's mouth.

"You are not smiling, Teacher," she said. "What is wrong?"

Miss Sullivan was glad Helen could not see the tears in her eyes. "I was just wishing Jimmie could have seen a circus," she told her.

Helen knew all about Jimmie, who had been Miss Sullivan's little lame brother. He had died in a poorhouse when he was six years old. There had been nowhere else for the two children to go.

Miss Sullivan had lived on in the poorhouse for four years after Jimmie had died. She had almost gone blind. Then a kind man had discovered her and sent her to Perkins School, where she had secured help.

Helen grasped her teacher's hand. "I know how you feel," she said. "I wish that Jimmie could have been here too, but I'm glad that you and I could be here together."

North Again

MORE THAN A YEAR had come and gone since Anne Sullivan had arrived at Ivy Green. Today she and Helen were spending the day at Keller's Landing on the Tennessee River.

This landing was a deserted wharf at the far end of the Keller farm. Soldiers had used it during the War between the States. Today it was a favorite picnic spot for Helen and Miss Sullivan, whom Helen now called "Teacher."

The April weather was warm and mild. Spring had come early. Helen started to gather smooth stones to build a dam on the dry bed of the creek. Then she knelt down to put the stones in place, one over another. When she had finished the dam, she reached out for Teacher's hand and gave it a familiar tug.

In reply Miss Sullivan spelled d-a-m. Helen nodded. Teacher had spelled to her about building the dam. Now it was her turn to spell.

"D-o-n-e," she spelled with her fingers.

The sun was high in the sky. Helen was tired and sleepy. Now that she had finished the dam, she was ready for something else. She felt her stomach and spelled, "L-u-n-c-h."

Miss Sullivan laughed. "L-i-t-t-l-e- p-i-g," she replied, pushing out the lunch basket.

Helen giggled. She knew all about little pigs. One day Miss Sullivan had seized a squealing piglet from the old sow's litter and placed it in Helen's hands. Helen would never forget the name of this plump, little animal that had wriggled so hard to get away. Nor had she forgotten other words, such as p-u-p-p-y, c-a-l-f, r-a-b-b-i-t,

90

s-q-u-i-r-r-e-l, k-i-t-t-e-n, f-i-s-h. The list grew rapidly every day.

Helen eagerly removed the napkin from their lunch basket. She raised the basket gently to her nose and sniffed. M-m-m-m! She could smell some sandwiches. She reached in the basket and sniffed again. She could smell boiled eggs, tomatoes, and chocolate pies.

Even though Helen was very hungry, she extended the basket politely to Miss Sullivan. This act was very pleasing to the teacher. A little more than a year before Helen had eaten almost like an animal. Today she realized that she should share her food with other people.

"I've known seven-year-olds with good eyes and ears who haven't learned to share," said Miss Sullivan. She handed Helen a sandwich and and took one for herself. Then they sat in the warm Alabama sunshine and munched away.

As Miss Sullivan ate, she thought about letters

she had received from Mr. Anagnos, the head of Perkins School. Captain Keller had received a letter from him, too.

"Helen, would you like to go on a trip with me?" she spelled into her young pupil's hand. Then she waited for the answer.

Helen's face shone. She loved the word g-o, and to go anywhere with Teacher would be exciting. "Y-e-s," she spelled.

Miss Sullivan's eyes danced. She was elated to observe the zest with which Helen had answered. Now the time had come, she felt, to have a little conversation with the girl. She sat down beside her and started to "talk."

"Your parents and I have already talked about your going," she told Helen. "My friend Mr. Anagnos wants to see you. Your mother and Mildred will go with us, but first we will go to Washington to see Dr. Bell. Do you remember Dr. Bell?" Helen shook her head.

"He remembers you," said Miss Sullivan. "Your father and mother took you to see him a long time ago. He wants to see you again."

Helen wrinkled up her forehead. "Oh, yes," she exclaimed. "Now I remember. He had a big watch. I sat on his lap."

Miss Sullivan nodded. "And we will be in Washington when Grover Cleveland is inaugurated President," she continued.

Helen pulled at her companion's hand. "I-n-a-u-g—i-n-a-u-g—I can't spell it. How do you spell it? What does it mean?"

"I shouldn't use such a big word," Miss Sullivan replied with a laugh. "It means that the people of the United States will see Mr. Cleveland become President—for the second time."

"Why?" Helen asked.

"Because the people like him, Little Miss Question Box," Miss Sullivan answered.

Helen was taking in every word. She had even

forgotten to eat. She waited for the conversation to continue. "And then?" she asked.

"And then we will go to Perkins School in Boston," explained Miss Sullivan. "That's where the blind children live who sent you a doll."

The trip north on the railroad train was a real adventure for Helen. She remembered little or nothing of her earlier journey on a train. This time she and Miss Sullivan sat facing Mrs. Keller and Mildred in a car. On her lap she held her favorite doll Nancy, wearing a fine new dress and a ruffled sunbonnet.

Helen saw the passing country through her companion's eyes. The scene changed with every mile. There were fields of cotton. There was the same Tennessee River that passed by Keller's Landing. There were stops at many stations where passengers got on and off.

All the while Helen sat, clutching her doll. "You love her best of all your dolls, don't you?"

94

said Miss Sullivan. "After all, you have known her the longest."

In Washington, Dr. Bell gave the little party a warm welcome. He greeted Helen like an old friend. "You have done well with her," he said to Miss Sullivan. "Tell me about her."

Miss Sullivan was overcome by his praise. "I haven't anything special to tell," she stammered. "I just have a stubborn Irish nature that won't give up. And Helen is a very bright child."

Dr. Bell turned his keen gaze on Helen. "I'm sure she is," he said. "Now I have a surprise for all of you. President Cleveland will receive us at the White House tomorrow."

No one in the party ever forgot the quarter-hour with the President. It was a typically American scene. The Chief Executive found time during a busy day to see two women and two little girls who were perfect strangers. He was eager to welcome them at the request of his

friend, Dr. Alexander Graham Bell. Neither man dreamed that the blind girl would one day be received by kings and queens and heads of state.

Of course it was hard for Helen to understand

the importance of the visit. She liked the big man in the cutaway coat that felt so smooth and fine to her fingers. She sensed the gentleness of his hands and felt that he must be a very friendly and helpful person. Now she must wait for Teacher to explain everything to her.

Helen was very happy when the group returned to the hotel. That night she crawled into bed with a happy sigh. "President Cleveland is a very kind man," she said to the others before she drifted off to sleep.

When the train reached Boston, Helen and Mildred were fast asleep. Two porters carried them and their luggage to a waiting carriage. Miss Sullivan and Mrs. Keller climbed inside with the sleepy children and the driver shook the reins over the horse's back. Then the weary travelers rattled away toward Perkins School.

Helen never knew when Miss Sullivan undressed her and tucked her into bed between snowy sheets. The morning sun was streaming in the windows when she awoke. Already a group of children had come to her room to welcome her. They looked over at her, calling various kinds of greetings.

"Welcome to Perkins, Helen."

"We are glad you have come!"

"She can't hear you," explained Miss Sullivan. "You must use sign language with her."

By now Helen was sitting straight up in bed, wearing a white ruffled nightdress. Her soft golden hair fell down over her shoulders. Her smile grew wider and wider as her new friends stepped forward one by one.

At first the children were shy about talking with her in sign language, but they soon began to talk freely and gayly. "You will like our swings and seesaws," said one of the girls.

Before long a freckle-faced boy with two missing front teeth slipped over to her side. "I have a present for you," he spelled. He poured a little stream of marbles into her hand. She rolled them about and liked their smooth surfaces.

Helen liked the friendly people at the Perkins School, including both children and adults. She could stay only a short time, because the school year was almost over. Soon most of the children would be going home for the summer.

The commencement exercises at the school were held in early June. Helen was allowed to sit on the stage with Miss Sullivan. Already, without knowing it, she was becoming famous.

When the school closed, Miss Sullivan and Helen took Mother and Mildred to board a train for Alabama. They planned to follow in a few weeks, but first they would visit Mrs. Hopkins, the school matron. She had invited them to come for a visit at her home on Cape Cod.

Mrs. Hopkins lived in the little town of Brewster on Cape Cod. Helen immediately fell in love with the big, old two-story frame house with large rooms and high ceilings.

The house contained many interesting things which had come from other parts of the world. There were ivory elephants. There was a music box. There was a set of Dutch China. There was a slippery haircloth sofa. Mrs. Hopkins allowed Helen to feel of all these things. Then Miss Sullivan told her about them.

Helen even went swimming while she was visiting the seashore. Miss Sullivan helped her put on a bathing suit and led her out the back door onto the beach. The house was located close beside the water.

Helen drew in a long breath of the fresh sea air. She had noticed the smell of this air when she had first come here, but today it seemed stronger and more delightful than ever. She dropped Miss Sullivan's hand and ran in the warm sand which felt good to her feet.

She stopped for a moment as she stepped into the shallow water. Then she ran forward as fast as she could. Miss Sullivan was close behind her, but had never dreamed that the child could run so fast. "Wait, dear!" she called.

By now a great wave was coming toward the shore. It swept over them as Miss Sullivan was trying to reach Helen. Then a few seconds later it threw them back on the sand. Miss Sullivan wiped her eyes and looked to see whether Helen was hurt or frightened.

Helen did not like the ocean water. She angrily tried to shake the water off her swimming suit. Then she began to spell rapidly. Miss Sullivan laughed as she read the words. "Who put salt in the water?" Helen demanded.

Pupil at Perkins

A YEAR had passed and once more Helen and Miss Sullivan were in the South. Helen now found learning an adventure and she was learning by leaps and bounds. There always were books to read, places to go, and things to do.

Helen wrote many letters in Braille, the system of writing used by the blind. She had a long list of friends to whom she wrote. There was Mr. Anagnos, who was soon going to Europe for a year. There were Dr. Alexander Graham Bell and Dr. Edward Everett Hale, a noted preacher, who was a distant cousin of the Kellers. Then there were all the children at Perkins School.

One great disappointment had come to Helen during the year. Miss Sullivan had gone north during the summer to see doctors about her eyes. Helen had blinked back tears when she had gone to the little train station to see her off.

"I musn't let her see me cry," she had told herself. "She might decide not to go, and that would never do. I shall miss her every minute, but I'll manage somehow."

The train had pulled away with Miss Sullivan aboard, and Helen had felt an ache in her throat. Life would be dull without Teacher.

The summer had passed better than Helen had expected. Her friends and family had been a great help to her. She had spent a great deal of time helping to look after her younger sister Mildred, who now got into all kinds of mischief. Then she had helped to care for a new baby brother, who had been named Phillips Brooks after a prominent American clergyman.

Now Miss Sullivan was back, but she did not expect to stay long. She planned to return to Boston and take Helen along to become a pupil at Perkins School. "You'll have a great time there," she said to Helen, "and all your friends will be happy to see you."

Within a few weeks Helen and Miss Sullivan were located at Perkins School. Helen took to her work in the school as a duck takes to water. She joined the other children excitedly in their work and play. She learned to read harder and harder books in Braille. She loved the well-stocked library and spent many hours there engrossed in her studies.

One day the eight-year-old girl wrote a letter to her parents at home!

"Clifton did not kiss me because he does not like to kiss little girls. He is shy. I am glad that Frank and Clarence and Robbie and Eddie and Charles and George are not very shy."

Helen's parents laughed when they read her words. "I can hardly believe that this is our child," said Mrs. Keller. "Do you remember what she was like before Miss Sullivan came?"

Mr. Keller nodded. "We owe that young woman a debt we can never repay," he said.

Helen and Miss Sullivan had many friends outside of Perkins School. They often visited the Chamberlin family about twenty-five miles from Boston. The Chamberlins with their children lived in an old farmhouse near King Philip's Pond. King Philip had been an Indian warrior when the Pilgrims landed at Plymouth.

During one weekend visit there was a heavy snowstorm. The wind outside howled and the air was crisp and cold. Whenever anyone opened a door, cold air rushed in.

The Chamberlins and their guests gathered in front of the big fireplace in the living room. They piled logs on the fire and felt safe and happy. They popped corn and roasted apples. They laughed and talked and sang. Helen had never been happier in her life.

When they went up to bed that night, Miss Sullivan told Helen about the blanket of snow that covered everything. She knew little about snow, because in Alabama snow usually melts almost as soon as it falls.

Next morning the young Chamberlins could talk of nothing but tobogganing. They wanted to go out at once. They said the snow might melt. Mr. Chamberlin laughed. "No danger of that. This snow is here to stay for awhile." He turned to Miss Sullivan. "Shall we take Helen?"

Miss Sullivan's eyes twinkled. "Yes, you couldn't very well leave her here. Sometimes I think that child's middle name is *go*."

Everyone dressed in warm clothes. They took the toboggan to the top of a high hill. Helen stooped down to feel the sled. It was flat on the

106

ground. It was long and smooth with a front end that curled upward. "It is dark green with red trimming," explained Miss Sullivan.

When they reached the top of the hill, everyone piled on. They were crowded together like sardines. Helen snuggled back against Miss Sullivan. The eldest Chamberlin boy shoved them and off they went.

Down, down, down sped the toboggan, and Helen was thrilled. She never had experienced anything like this in Alabama. The cold wind rushed against her cheeks and took her breath away. "This must be how the birds feel!" she thought.

At last the toboggan came to a stop on level ground and the passengers scrambled to their feet. Helen turned and walked away. "Where is she going?" asked Mr. Chamberlin.

Miss Sullivan wondered too, but soon started to laugh. There Helen went with one hand

107

pointing to the top of the hill from which they had come. "She wants to go again," Miss Sullivan explained to the others.

By now it was almost time for Christmas. "This will be the first Christmas I have ever spent away from home," said Helen.

"We have much to do before Christmas," reminded Miss Sullivan. "There are only ten shopping days left. Mrs. Hopkins wants us to pick out gifts for all the younger children at school."

That afternoon Helen tucked her arm in Miss Sullivan's arm to go shopping in Boston. They went up and down one street after another in the shopping district.

Helen spelled so fast that Miss Sullivan could hardly keep up with her. In the first store they entered, they walked past a perfume counter. Helen sniffed eagerly. She recognized a delicate scent of lilacs in the air.

"That perfume makes me think of home," she

announced. "It smells like the lilac bush by our back door. Isn't it wonderful!"

"Yes, and very expensive," Miss Sullivan added, "but we can enjoy smelling it."

"Do you like it?" Helen asked.

"I love it!" replied Miss Sullivan. "When I was a small girl, I lived in a poor neighborhood where people had no money to purchase perfumes. Often we did not have enough to eat."

Miss Sullivan wondered whether Helen was listening, because already she was tugging to go on to the next counter, but Helen had listened. She felt sorry for Teacher and read into Teacher's words a longing for beautiful things she had never owned. Somehow she held tighter to the red leather purse which she carried in her hand. This purse contained a generous check for Christmas that she had received in the mail from her father earlier in the day.

"This money should cover your Christmas

shopping," Helen's father had written. "Your mother sent you a box yesterday with many surprises in it, but this money is from me. After you finish buying gifts for others, there should be something left. Use whatever is left to buy something special for yourself. From your father who will miss you on Christmas morning."

Next Helen and Miss Sullivan stopped at a store that sold all sorts of toys. There were dolls and doll furniture, such as beds, chairs, sofas, and tables. There were large and small doll houses. There were blocks and games and balls and wind-up animals. There were stuffed animals of all sizes and shapes. Helen held them to her face and stroked their soft fur.

"We should get this doll for Susie," she said, picking up a small doll in a cradle. Then she put the doll down. "No, I think she would rather have this Scotch boy in kilts," she spelled plainly to her teacher.

Miss Sullivan translated for the sales lady, who looked surprised. "She understands more with her fingers than most of us see with our eyes or hear with our ears," she said to the sales lady.

At last their shopping was completed. There were gifts for Susie, Mary, Sadie, Dan, Clifton, Frank, Clarence, Robbie, Eddie, Charles and all the others. There was a water color for Mrs. Hopkins and leather note pad for Mr. Anagnos. There was a pot of bright red flowers for the cook's kitchen window.

Helen and Miss Sullivan finished the afternoon in a little tea shop where someone gently played Christmas music. Helen could not hear the music, but she could feel the beat.

For a moment as they sipped hot chocolate and munched little cakes, Miss Sullivan wished that Helen could see. She wished that Helen could see firsthand the appealing holiday decorations. Then she looked at Helen's glowing face and realized that sight would add nothing to her enjoyment. "You are a pleasure to take shopping," she spelled into Helen's hand.

Helen's mouth gave a mischievous little twist. She had a secret, which she wanted to keep from Teacher and everybody else.

A week before Christmas, workmen dragged a great, fragrant, dark-green cedar tree into the center hall at Perkins School. The children stood at a safe distance to watch the men work.

The smaller children gathered around Helen and she told them a story. "Once that big tree grew in a great forest on a mountain," she said. "The warm sun shone on it. The winds blew on it. The birds built nests in its branches. The mother birds laid eggs in the nests. Soon the little birds hatched."

From her chair near the fireplace Miss Sullivan smiled. Only yesterday she had read Helen

112

a story from Hans Christian Anderson. Now she wanted others to enjoy the story.

Helen was holding the children spellbound. When she said the word *eggs*, she made a little circle with her thumb and forefinger. She was so full of life that she used her hands even when she was not spelling.

The eldest child in the group held his hand over Helen's as she told the story. Then he repeated it to the others in her exact words. The children listened closely.

"The little birds hatched," Helen told them. "For a while they flew back and forth among the branches. Then they grew up and flew away. The father and mother birds left, too. They all flew south. The tree was lonely for them. Then one day men came with axes. They chopped away at the tree."

"Did they hurt the tree?" asked a round-faced youngster. "Did they hurt it?"

"Certainly not," Helen told him. "The tree knew it was coming to Perkins School to spend Christmas with us. It knew we would trim it with colored balls and gold chains and shining tinsel and popcorn balls——"

The children jumped up and down. "We want to begin! We want to trim the tree now!"

Miss Sullivan and the other teachers hurried to spread newspapers on the floor. They set out jars of paste and handed out blunt scissors and sheets of red and green and gold and silver paper. They seemed to have everything.

The busy group of children cut and pasted and laughed and chattered all afternoon. A stranger happening in would never have guessed at first that they were blind children.

Several of them shook corn poppers over the glowing coals. The little yellow kernels turned to big white fluffy pieces under the magic of the heat. Other children took the pieces and strung them into long chains to hang on the tree. Helen's chain was the longest one.

Soon the day passed and it was dark outside. Miss Sullivan placed a big bowl of hot buttered popcorn in the middle of the floor. Then she called to the children calmly: "It's time to clean up. Gather up the scraps of paper. Drop the scissors into the box which Helen is holding. Stack up the unused paper. We will want it tomorrow. Work is over for the day. When you have finished your chores, make a circle. Then I will pass the popcorn. Do you want Helen to tell you another story?"

"Yes!" they shouted at the tops of their voices. They scampered about like elves. In the twinkling of an eye they were greasy and happy with popcorn. They sat down in a circle and waited eagerly for Helen to begin.

"Once upon a time," Helen began to say happily on her fingers to a boy whose hand was touching hers. Then she told everybody the story of Little Red Riding Hood.

Christmas morning dawned cold and clear, and all the children at Perkins School were up early. All of them, including Helen, had hung up their stockings.

Helen had awakened long before Teacher and was sitting up in bed. Her face was rosy with excitement. She was shaking the last bit of candy from her Christmas stocking. Any artist would have enjoyed painting her picture.

"Everything I want! Braille books from Mother and Father, a new dress from Cousin Ev, a pine-needle pillow from Mildred, fudge from Viney, and this precious doll from you. This is the happiest Christmas of my life, Teacher."

Breakfast was a hasty affair. Everyone was too excited to eat. At eleven o'clock the children settled down to hear the Reverend Phillips Brooks, a Boston pastor and their good friend.

He was a tall, broad-shouldered man with snow-white hair and a handsome face. Teacher spelled his words into Helen's hand.

"So remember on Christmas Day that God gave His greatest gift to you—because God is Love," he finished.

The chimes sounded for dinner. The children found their places at the tables in the dining room for a gay meal. Each child had a paper cracker that snapped when it was pulled and produced a silly little hat. The blind children laughed heartily when they put on the hats.

"What kind of hat is mine, Teacher?" asked Helen. "Please tell me what kind I have."

"You have a policeman's hat," said Miss Sullivan. "Sallie has a sailor's cap. I never saw so many different kinds of hats."

Soon the food was served, and eating put an end to the talk. The plates were filled with turkey and dressing and mashed potatoes with rich gravy. The children ate and ate until they were stuffed. They could hardly find room for the mince pies that followed.

At last the day drew to a close. Helen, wearing a red robe, sat in the bedroom which she shared with Teacher. She was sleepy, but she hated for Christmas to end.

The excited girl had saved her greatest enjoyment for the last. Now just before going to bed, she gave Teacher a little wooden box, containing a tiny vial of lilac perfume, which she and Mrs. Hopkins had purchased together. She couldn't see how joyfully surprised Miss Sullivan was as she opened the tissue-wrapped package, but she felt it in the warm hug that followed. "How did you do it, Helen?" asked Teacher. "How in the world did you manage?"

Helen tossed her head saucily. "There are ways and ways," she replied. "A person doesn't always need eyes to get things done."

119

Helen Learns to Speak

HELEN and Miss Sullivan were back at Perkins School for the third year. By now Helen was ten years old, and each year she had learned very fast. No other pupil in the school had learned so fast or so well.

One afternoon after school when Helen went to her bedroom, she found Miss Sullivan talking with a strange lady. "This is Mrs. Lamson," Miss Sullivan explained to Helen. "Once she was a teacher here at Perkins School."

Helen liked the new woman almost at once. She liked the friendly touch of her fingers and the sweet scent of perfume on her clothes. Most of all Helen liked her words when she said, "I feel as though I'm coming home here."

Mrs. Lamson kept on talking. She talked directly to Miss Sullivan and in sign language to Helen. "I have just returned from Norway, where I met a deaf and blind girl who could talk," she said. "I found her so interesting that I want to tell you about her."

Mrs. Lamson went on. "This girl learned to speak with her lips. I could hardly believe it at first; but it was really true."

Helen quivered with excitement. How would it feel to speak? She had felt her friends' lips move as they talked and had longed to talk herself. When she was a small girl, she had moved her lips and wondered why nothing happened. This girl had learned the magic of speech.

"I'm sure I could teach Helen to speak," said Miss Sullivan, "but I wouldn't know where to start. I wish I knew how."

"You won't have to know, at least not in the beginning," said Mrs. Lamson, "because a fine teacher lives right here in Boston. I came to tell you about her. Her name is Miss Sarah Fuller, and she is principal of Horace Mann School for the Deaf."

"I want to meet her!" Helen spelled out furiously. "Please take me to her. I want to learn to speak right away. If the girl in Norway could learn, I can learn, too."

A few days later Miss Sullivan and Helen waited for Miss Fuller in the parlor at the Horace Mann School. Miss Sullivan was as excited as Helen over the prospect of Helen's learning to talk. They had lost no time in coming.

Soon a tall, stylish lady with a queenly air came down the hall and entered the room. She had a confident look about her, as if she could accomplish almost anything. Miss Sullivan wished that Helen could see her.

"I am Sarah Fuller," said the woman, holding out her hand. "You must be Anne Sullivan and this must be Helen Keller."

Miss Sullivan reached for Miss Fuller's hand. "We have come," she said, "to find out whether

123

you can teach Helen to speak. She wants to speak more than anything else in the world."

"I'll be happy to try," said Miss Fuller. "I have taught many others." She began to spell into Helen's hand, "G-o-o-d m-o-r-n-i-n-g, H-e-l-e-n. I a-m M-i-s-s F-u-l-l-e-r."

"G-o-o-d m-o-r-n-i-n-g, M-i-s-s F-u-l-l-e-r," Helen returned politely.

"D-o y-o-u w-i-s-h t-o l-e-a-r-n t-o s-p-e-a-k?" asked Miss Fuller.

Helen's face shone. "O-h, p-l-e-a-s-e!"

Miss Fuller looked at Miss Sullivan and said, "She is a very bright little girl."

"She is the brightest child for her age that I have ever known," replied Miss Sullivan. "Do you think she can learn to speak?"

All the while Miss Fuller had been watching Helen closely. "I think that she can," she said thoughtfully. "I really think so."

Miss Fuller again put Helen's hand over her

own and began to use the manual alphabet. "Tell me your favorite word, my dear."

Helen smiled. "T-e-a-c-h-e-r," she replied, slipping a hand into Miss Sullivan's.

"Listen carefully," said Miss Fuller, "while I say *teacher* with my lips. I shall say it several times. Place your middle finger on my nose, your forefinger on my lips, and your thumb on my chin. Feel how the word sounds."

Helen obeyed. Miss Fuller spoke the word several times. She spoke it clearly. "Now say it," she told Helen.

Miss Sullivan almost held her breath. Helen opened her lips and tried but gave out only a meaningless sound. She tried again, but once more gave out a meaningless sound.

Miss Fuller did not seem discouraged. She gave Helen a farewell pat. "Bring her on Mondays and Thursdays for a few weeks," she said to Miss Sullivan. "Then we'll see what she can do."

Helen, accompanied by Miss Sullivan, went to Miss Fuller for eleven lessons. In the first lesson she learned the *m* sound by pressing her lips together. She learned the *t* sound by pressing her upper teeth with her tongue. She learned other sounds including *p, a, s,* and *i.*

Miss Fuller was delighted with Helen, who constantly learned something new. Every day Helen practiced with Teacher. It was hard to tell which one worked harder.

Miss Sullivan and Miss Fuller understood each other. They smiled across Helen every time she learned a new sound. They were elated when she spoke her first sentence, "It-is-warm."

"I am very proud of you," Miss Sullivan spelled happily into Helen's hand.

Helen smiled. "Now I can talk to my sister," she spelled. "Won't she be surprised?"

At the end of eleven lessons Miss Fuller turned Helen over to Miss Sullivan. "You can teach her now," she said. "I will give you all the help I can. There are several books you can get. She is ready to go fast now."

Miss Fuller took Helen's hand and spelled, "You have learned a great deal during these lessons. You must keep on learning. From now on Miss Sullivan will teach you. She knows how and can help you. I have watched her. She has worked as hard as you have."

Helen thought for a moment as the words sank into her mind. She opened her arms wide and tried to hug both women at once. Somehow she wanted both of the women to share her great happiness in learning to speak.

"I-am-not-dumb-now," Helen said in the tone of the deaf who have learned to speak. "I-am-not-dumb-now. I can speak."

The Railroad Trestle

THE KELLER FAMILY was spending a month at Fern Quarry, their summer cottage in the mountains. This summer home was fourteen miles from Ivy Green, where they lived.

Helen loved every moment there. She loved the gentle breezes that rustled through the trees. She loved the autumn leaves that came drifting down. She loved the squirrels that scampered from branch to branch in the trees.

"The squirrels make odd little noises, when they are fussing at one another," her sister Mildred explained to her. Mildred was getting to be a big girl. She tagged along everywhere after

Helen. She was wonderful company. The sisters spent much of their time together whenever Helen was home from school.

People were always coming and going at Fern Quarry. Often Mr. Keller's friends came to go hunting with him. On many mornings Helen was awakened by the smell of coffee and frying ham. Then she felt the men's heavy tread as they left with their guns and dogs.

While they were gone, the servants prepared a barbecue. Helen squatted by the long deep hole which the men servants dug in the ground. She waited by the side while they made a fire at the bottom of the pit to roast the meat. She loved to feel the heat coming up from below.

"Be careful, Helen," her mother said.

Miss Sullivan never told Helen to be careful. She wanted Helen to know about everything, but she was always near in case of danger. Usually Helen did not know she was near.

After the men servants built the fire in the pit, they placed iron bars across the top. Then they strung pieces of pork or veal on wires and hung them from the rods over the fire. The meat roasted for several hours over the fire, until it became tender and juicy.

Once Helen was allowed to prepare a piece of raw meat for the barbecue. She pushed some wire through the meat and fastened the wire to a rod over the fire, just as the servants had done. "Now!" she exclaimed, sitting back on her heels. "I am a barbecue cook, too."

There were many pleasures at Fern Quarry. One day Mr. Keller brought a new pony to the cottage. Helen named it Black Beauty after the pony in her favorite book. She rode Black Beauty hours at a time with Miss Sullivan holding the reins.

Sometimes when there was little danger, Miss Sullivan would drop the rein. Then Black

130

Beauty would ramble along with Helen on his back. He seemed to enjoy these times as much as Helen. Often he stopped to nibble grass.

There was a railroad track about a mile from Fern Quarry extending through the mountains. At one spot it crossed a deep ravine before it reached the other side. Helen had heard many tales from Mildred and others about the long railroad trestle across the deep ravine. She almost shuddered as they described it.

"The ties are this far apart," said Mildred, stretching out her small arms for Helen to feel. "I don't even like to look at them."

"They are narrow, too," added Percy. "They are so narrow you almost cut your feet when you try to walk on them."

Martha Washington shivered. "They're a long way from the ground. You won't catch me walking on them. No, sir-r-e-e!"

Early one October afternoon Miss Sullivan,

131

Helen, and Mildred started out for a walk in the woods. It was a beautiful day with a hint of frost in the air. The trees were tinged with red as Helen and Mildred scampered along.

More than an hour passed after they left the cottage. After a while they came upon a grove of pecan trees. An early frost had caused many nuts to drop to the ground. Helen and Mildred ran about and piled them in heaps.

"We will come back with Black Beauty to-morrow," said Miss Sullivan. "All those nuts are too heavy for us to carry now."

She looked at her watch. "It is nearly four o'clock," she said. "We should start home."

At once she stood up and looked about to see which way to go. Then she realized that they had wandered off the trail. She spelled into Helen's hand, "I am not certain which way to go. I did not know when we left the trail, and I cannot find it. I'm afraid we are lost."

132

Helen had an odd feeling. She couldn't imagine Teacher being lost, even in the mountains. Soon she felt little Mildred pulling at her side and sobbing. She stooped and put her arms about the frightened child. "There, there, little sister," she comforted. "You mustn't cry. Teacher and I will take care of you."

Miss Sullivan threw a glance at Helen and noted that her face was serene and untroubled. She realized that Helen trusted her and wished that she trusted herself as much.

They started off with Miss Sullivan leading the way and Helen and Mildred following. They looked closely for the trail that would lead them back to Fern Quarry. There was little time for talking. All were calm except Mildred who still gave a little sniffle now and then.

Miss Sullivan continued to walk in front through the thick underbrush. Helen was sure she would find the trail sooner or later. "I won't bother her by asking questions," she said. "She has all she can do to get us home."

For a long time they walked. The woods seemed endless. The bushes scratched their arms and legs. At last Mildred became tired and they had to stop to rest.

The sun started to go down and the air grew chilly. The nights had been cool for a long time. Before long it would be dark. The mountain was a lonely place, especially at night, except for foxes and wildcats that roamed about.

"Look there!" cried Mildred pointing.

"Look at what?" asked Miss Sullivan, peering ahead. "What do you see?"

Mildred jumped up and down clapping her hands. "The trestle! There's the trestle!"

There it was, indeed. Miss Sullivan looked at the two girls. One was blind and the other was only seven years old. Her own eyes were none too good. What should she do now?

The ravine lay between them and the trail that led home. When they reached that trail, they could easily find their way home, but first they would have to cross that dangerous trestle. If they made one misstep, they would fall three hundred feet to the rocks below.

Miss Sullivan looked back the way they had come. She realized that she could not retrace their steps with the darkness of night fast approaching. Calmly she sat down on a fallen log and drew Helen close to her. Then she wrote into Helen's hand, choosing her words carefully. She did not want to frighten the child. Yet she must make her understand.

When Miss Sullivan finished talking, Helen nodded. She trusted Teacher. She would try to be brave for the sake of little Mildred who still was showing signs of fright. "Come, dear," she said, holding out her hand to Mildred. "Teacher and I will get you safely home."

In a short time the three were at the edge of the trestle. Miss Sullivan was glad that Helen could not see how old and unsafe the structure looked. Helen gave Teacher's hand a little pull. "When do we start across?" she asked.

Miss Sullivan brushed aside her fear. "I'll go first and hold your hand every step of the way. Then you hold Mildred's hand and don't let loose for a second. Make your way slowly and carefully from one beam to another."

The trio started out. As they went far out on the trestle, Miss Sullivan was encouraged by the firm clasp of Helen's hand. She knew that Helen was holding fast to her sister's hand just as firmly. When they reached the middle of the trestle all of them felt somewhat relaxed. Soon they would reach the other side.

Then suddenly everything changed. There was the shrill sound of a train whistle in the distance. Soon a train would come rolling over the

trestle from the mountains. Helen felt the rever-
beration and knew what it meant. Miss Sullivan
gave Helen's hand a tug. They must hurry to get
across before the train came.

"I can't move any faster," said Helen. "Mildred won't budge. I think she is frozen to the
spot, Teacher."

Miss Sullivan threw Mildred a despairing
glance. The child seemed rooted to a trestle tie.
She was too frightened to move a single step.
The approaching train gave another whistle,
and Helen pulled at Miss Sullivan's hand. "Are
there supports under the tracks?" she asked.
"Can we climb down on some supports?"

Miss Sullivan glanced down. At first she grew
dizzy as she saw the rocks far below. Then she
opened her eyes again and looked for the supports. There they were a few feet below the
tracks, just as Helen had thought they might be.
Without seeing them, she knew that the trestle

138

would have crossbraces. Now could they safely climb down and reach the crossbraces in time? One thing was certain. Every other path of escape was closed. Another blast sounded from the oncoming train. Already smoke could be seen curling up above the treetops.

"Follow me," she spelled into Helen's hand. "Hold on to Mildred." Then with a silent prayer she climbed down to the crossbraces and helped Helen to climb down beside her. All the while she tried to look out for little Mildred to make certain she would not become hysterical.

Soon the train rolled onto the trestle. The engineer and the passengers did not dream that three terror-stricken persons were clinging to a narrow support below them.

The train roared above them like a mighty monster and caused the trestle to shake and tremble. The smoke nearly choked them. Sparks and bits of glowing coal fell all about them.

Somehow they made their way back to the top of the trestle. Then they proceeded nervously from tie to tie on across to pick up their trail. By this time it was completely dark, but they cautiously felt their way down the mountainside.

At last they saw lights coming around a bend in the trail. Captain Keller had organized a search party to hunt for them. Now he came on the run, eager to take his two daughters into his arms. He held them both close and said, "Thank God we've found you. I was beginning to think we never would."

Helen slipped a hand into her father's hand and spelled out, "Why, Father, you shouldn't have been worried. You might have known that Teacher would bring us home safe and sound."

The Frost King

"WHAT can I send Mr. Anagnos for his birthday?" Helen asked Teacher.

"I think he would like something you have made," Miss Sullivan replied.

Helen looked thoughtful. "All the children at Perkins School make things for him. He couldn't ever use all the drawings, penwipers, and blotters he gets." Then she clapped her hands. "I know! I know what I'll send him."

"What?" asked Miss Sullivan curiously.

Helen drew a long breath and smiled mysteriously. "I'll show it to you after I make it. I want to make it all by myself."

By now Helen and Miss Sullivan were back in Alabama for the summer vacation. In the autumn they would return to Perkins School, and Helen would be with blind children again.

The walls of Ivy Green were almost bursting with children. Besides Helen and Mildred, there was little Phillips Brooks, who toddled about and got in everybody's way. In addition there were numerous cousins, who came for short visits. The children went everywhere, playing games of hide-and-seek and tag. Helen ran and played as hard as any of the others.

Even though Helen had fun, she did not forget Mr. Anagnos' birthday. Every day she shut herself in her room for an hour or so to work on his present. All the while she kept the present a secret from Teacher and all the others.

At last she brought a little pile of sheets neatly written in script for the blind. She showed them to Teacher and said shyly, "I have written a little story for Mr. Anagnos, called 'The Frost King.' Would you like to read it?"

"Of course I would," said Miss Sullivan.

Helen handed over the sheets and waited and wondered while Miss Sullivan read the story to herself. She had worked very hard writing the story and wondered whether Teacher would like it and whether Mr. Anagnos would like it.

As she waited, she thought of certain pleasing groups of words in the story: "in a beautiful palace far to the north—a thousand glittering spires—twelve soldierly-looking bears." She had written as well as she could.

At last Miss Sullivan laid down the sheets. She took both of Helen's hands in hers and held them tightly for a moment. Then she began to write into Helen's hand a very pleasing message, "Your story makes me extremely happy. No teacher ever had such a fine pupil. Mr. Anagnos will like his birthday present very much."

Of course Captain and Mrs. Keller read the story. The captain read it aloud to Mildred. She looked wide-eyed at Helen and placed a finger solemnly on her sister's arm.

"What's that for?" asked Helen.

Teacher laughed. "She says she wants to touch you. She thinks you are a great writer."

That afternoon Helen and Teacher addressed and mailed a large brown envelope to Mr. Anagnos. Included in the envelope was the beautiful story which Helen had written. Soon she received a letter from Mr. Anagnos thanking her and saying that he, too, was very proud of her.

The good times continued at Ivy Green. At last the summer vacation was over, and Helen and Teacher went north again. By now Helen was beginning to feel almost as much at home in Boston as in Tuscumbia. The fall months passed quickly and it was time to celebrate Christmas and New Year's at Perkins School.

Helen now lived in a room by herself at the school. One morning in January she arose early, took her bath, and dressed by the crackling fire. The weather was cold, and she could feel the icy air creeping in around the windows. By now she had learned to like the cold northern weather. It made her want to be up and doing.

Suddenly she felt Teacher's hand on hers. Usually she did not get to see Miss Sullivan until after breakfast in the morning. At once she was disturbed and wondered what had happened. "What is wrong?" she asked eagerly.

Teacher took Helen's hands in hers. "I have some bad news for you," she replied.

Helen grew cold with fear. "Is Father or Mother or someone else in the family ill?"

"Oh, no," Miss Sullivan replied quickly. "Do you remember your story, 'The Frost King'?"

"Yes, of course I do," replied Helen.

Miss Sullivan hesitated. "Well, Mr. Anagnos

had the story published, and now people are saying that it was written years ago by a lady named Miss Canby."

Helen's face flushed. "But, Teacher, I wrote the story. I worked on it all summer."

Miss Sullivan put an arm around Helen. "I

know you wrote it, dear, but people say the two stories are very much alike."

Helen raised a troubled face as Teacher went on. "Certain expressions in the stories are very much alike. Is it possible that you could have heard Miss Canby's story somewhere and have remembered it?"

"Read me the lady's story," Helen begged. "Let me hear it for myself."

Miss Sullivan sat down and opened the magazine in her hand. Slowly she began to spell the words into her pupil's hand. " 'King Frost, or Jack Frost as he is sometimes called, lives in a cold country far to the North—' "

"I like my beginning better," spelled Helen. " 'King Frost lives in a beautiful palace far to the North in a land of perpetual snow—' "

The flames leaped in the fireplace, and the room became very still. Miss Sullivan went on reading and spelling words into Helen's hand.

At last she finished and dropped the magazine to the floor. Helen's face was unhappy. "Did Miss Canby write her story first?" she asked.

"Yes," answered Miss Sullivan. "There is no doubt that the stories are alike, but many expressions in your story are your own. Now where could you possibly have heard Miss Canby's story 'The Frost Fairies'? I never read it to you."

"My story is a child's story, Teacher. I thought about it last year after you told me how beautiful the woods were near the river. I did not copy Miss Canby's story to write my own. Truly I didn't."

"I'm sure you didn't," said Miss Sullivan. Helen gave a little sob. "I wouldn't copy, Teacher. It wouldn't be honest, and you have always taught me to be honest."

"You are honest," Miss Sullivan told her. "You are the most honest person I know."

Soon Helen was called to Mr. Anagnos' office where she was questioned by a group of people. Four of the persons were blind, and four of them were not. After they finished questioning, they still could not agree. Some believed that Helen had told the truth, and other did not. Some believed that Miss Sullivan had helped her.

The following days were very sad for Helen. She crept around the school like a little shadow. Her lessons suffered. Miss Sullivan longed to help her, but there was nothing she could do.

Finally people concluded that someone had told Helen the story years before. One day she was cheered by a letter from Miss Canby.

"I am a writer, and I understand what happened to you. You heard my story, tucked it away in your mind, and forgot it. When you wrote your story, you gave it some fine new touches. You improved my story. Do not feel troubled about it any more. I send you my warmest love."

Miss Sullivan folded the letter and put it back into the envelope. "There now," she said to Helen. "You can forget the whole affair and get back to your work in school."

Helen shook her head. "I can't do that. I don't think I ever want to write again. It might not be my own work."

"Nonsense," replied Miss Sullivan. "This same thing has happened to others. When you have something to say, you will write again."

Helen held out her hand. "Please give me the letter. I should like to keep it. Miss Canby must be a very nice lady."

"She must be," Miss Sullivan agreed. "Now you forget the matter and go back to your studies. You have been idle long enough."

A Time
to Remember

IT WAS LATE August, 1892. The family doctor in Tuscumbia had just given Helen a checkup. With a snap he closed his worn leather bag and said, "She's as sound as a dollar." Then he brought out a little paper sack and said, "Here, Helen. Have a peppermint."

The girl laughed as he spelled into her hand. "I'm not a baby any longer, Dr. Jackson," she said. "I'm twelve years old."

The doctor looked over his spectacles at her. "You are still my baby," he informed her. "Half the people here are my babies. I've given pills and powders to everyone under forty." He offered a peppermint to Miss Sullivan and said, "I'll claim you by adoption."

Miss Sullivan smiled and took a mint. "Thank you," she said graciously.

"Keep her at home for awhile," the old doctor advised, nodding his head at Helen. He turned to Miss Sullivan. "She looks a bit peaked," he explained. "Are you working her too hard?"

Miss Sullivan promptly replied, "You're mistaken. She works me. Every morning she wakes me up asking questions."

The doctor nodded. "I believe you, but slow her down for a while, if you can. We folks in Tuscumbia are mighty proud of both of you."

Helen and Miss Sullivan did not return to Perkins School that fall. The unfortunate affair about "The Frost King" had done its damage to both of them. Mr. Anagnos was no longer their friend. The present loving air of Ivy Green was good medicine for them.

In April, 1893, Captain Keller sent Helen and Miss Sullivan north to travel and visit friends. Dr. Alexander Graham Bell arranged for them to go to Rochester, New York, to visit a school for the deaf. One afternoon the three of them attended a tea which was given in Helen's honor by some of their friends.

When they returned to their hotel, Dr. Bell gave Miss Sullivan a sharp look and said, "You are tired. Go on to bed and rest. I promise to take good care of Helen."

Helen went with Dr. Bell willingly. She enjoyed being with him. That evening passers-by in the lobby turned their heads to look at the middle-aged gentleman and the pretty teen-aged girl beside him. Some of them envied the smiling young woman who looked so happy.

Dr. Bell sat in a big overstuffed chair in the lobby and Helen sat on the edge of another over-stuffed chair. She extended her hand to him so she could talk with him. Her cheeks were pink with excitement.

"You look like a princess," Dr. Bell said. "Would you like to make a wish?"

She shook her head. "I don't think so. I already have almost everything I want. I have Teacher, my family, and this trip."

"I have something to add," Dr. Bell told her. "How would you like to take Miss Sullivan to Niagara Falls? I would go with you."

Helen jumped from her chair and threw her arms about Dr. Bell's neck. "You are more than a prince! You are a fairy godfather."

Several persons passing by smiled at the simple, joyful act. Only a few realized that Helen was blind. Most of them saw only a happy, very much alive, young girl.

Soon the three friends visited Niagara Falls. Among all the visitors who came to this famed spot, Helen probably enjoyed its attraction most.

154

Clasping Miss Sullivan's hand tightly she felt with delight the plunging of the swirling waters. She went down a hundred and twenty feet in an elevator to a spot below the falls. She crossed over a suspension bridge to the Canadian side. All these wonders she remembered joyfully the rest of her life.

After more visits with friends Helen and Miss Sullivan went with Dr. Bell to the World's Columbian Exposition in Chicago. The president of the Exposition gave her a letter opening every door, and she entered every one.

She touched with loving hands the wonderful French bronzes. She rode on a camel in the Cairo sector. She traveled in a gondola on the replica of the lagoons of Venice. She held the Tiffany diamond valued at one hundred thousand dollars. She walked and walked, taking in more than most persons could see. Throughout life she happily remembered her trip here.

That same year Helen and Miss Sullivan boarded a railroad train for Hulton, a small town in Pennsylvania. "I shall be glad to get back to lessons," Helen declared. "It's time for me to get to work."

Miss Sullivan had arranged for Helen to study under a tutor in Hulton. She realized more and more that the girl needed someone with more education than she herself had. This new tutor had a rich educational background.

By now Helen was more eager than ever to learn, and Miss Sullivan was more eager to help her. One day when they were talking at Hulton, Helen surprised the teacher by announcing that she wanted to go to college.

"College!" exclaimed Miss Sullivan. "Do you think that is possible, my dear?"

Helen frowned. "Why not?" she demanded. "Aren't you always telling me to think? Doesn't college require people to think?"

Miss Sullivan waited briefly before answering. She didn't want to discourage Helen about her plans, but she wanted to help the girl realize some of the difficulties in her path. "College takes hard work," she said calmly. "College teachers cannot go slowly just for you."

"Then I will take twice as long to graduate," Helen said firmly. "My mind is made up, Teacher. I am going to college."

Miss Sullivan gave a little shrug. She realized that she herself was a strong-willed person, but she knew that she was no match for Helen. She would gain nothing by differing with the girl. Finally after a moment's pause she asked, "Where would you like to attend college?"

"At Radcliffe, Teacher. They say it's hard to be accepted there, hard to graduate from, but one of the best colleges in the whole country. I want to go to Radcliffe."

"Let's plan for you to go to Wright-Humason

School in New York first," Teacher suggested. "The work for the deaf at this school will help you. As you know, Mr. Spaulding will make it possible for you to go there."

Mr. Spaulding was a wealthy man in Boston. He was called the sugar king because he had made his money by dealing in sugar. "Yes, dear King John," cried Helen enthusiastically. "What a kind, generous man he is!"

Miss Sullivan smiled. "Many people are interested in you, Helen, and want to help you," she said. "They realize that you are handicapped and enjoy doing things for you."

"You do more than anyone else," said Helen. "I'm grateful to everyone, but most of all, I am grateful to you. I fully realize that I would be hopeless without you."

Helen attended the Wright-Humason school for a period of two years. She improved her speech somewhat, but still she and Miss Sullivan were dissatisfied. At last they decided to try another school.

The next year Helen enrolled at the Cambridge School for Young Ladies in Boston, where she hoped to prepare for Radcliffe College. When Christmas approached, she waited for her mother and Mildred to come for a visit. They had promised to spend Christmas with her.

Classes were over until after the holidays. Many of the girls had gone home. There would be plenty of room at Howells' House for Mrs. Keller and Mildred. "I have to pinch myself once in a while to be sure we are living in Mr. Howells' old home in Cambridge," said Helen.

Teacher smiled. "I am sure he wouldn't want you to do that."

"Do you mean live in his house?" Helen inquired with an innocent air.

"No, pinch yourself," said Teacher.

Helen laughed merrily. She was sitting on a

low stool by the fire, resting and thinking. She held her chin on her knees and stared ahead with her sightless eyes.

"We spent happy days in New York, didn't we?" she said. "And think of all the famous people we met at Aunt Eleanor Hutton's house. I'm glad she wanted me to call her 'Aunt Eleanor,' even if she isn't any kin to me."

Miss Sullivan almost said, "You must remember that you are a famous girl," but she pushed the words back. She wanted Helen to remain simple and unspoiled as she had been for years.

Helen began to call off the names of some of the famous people she knew. "I know Mary Mapes Dodge, John D. Rockefeller, Henry Van Dyke, Woodrow Wilson, Kate Douglas Wiggin, Joseph Jefferson, and Mark Twain," she said.

"Help!" Miss Sullivan exclaimed, laughing. "You sound as though you are calling the roll of Who's Who in America."

Helen's face was serious. "I realize they are important people, but they are good, kind people, too. If it weren't for many of them, we couldn't be here today."

By now Captain Keller had died and Helen was forced to depend on others for help. Miss Sullivan fully realized the circumstances and appreciated what others were doing. At the same time she did not want Helen to become spoiled.

"Aunt Eleanor is great," Helen went on. "She and others have raised enough money to see me through college. Isn't that wonderful?"

Miss Sullivan rose to her feet. "It certainly is," she said. "Now let's put on our wraps and walk down the street to meet your mother and Mildred. They should be arriving soon."

The Christmas season at Howells' House was a joyful event. Helen and Mildred had fun playing with the girls who lived too far away to go home for the holidays. They played games, made fudge, took long walks, had furious battles in the snow, and sat around the big fire in the living room. Helen had never been so happy in her life.

On the last night of vacation Helen seemed to lack some of her usual joyous spirit. "I hate to see tomorrow come," she said to her mother. "I know you must go home to Phillips, but I wish Mildred could stay here with me."

Miss Keller smiled at Miss Sullivan. "Shall I tell her?" she asked.

"Why not?" Miss Sullivan replied.

Mrs. Keller spelled rapidly into Helen's hand. "We have a surprise. Mildred has a scholarship here and can stay with you until summer."

Helen sprang to her feet, filled with excitement. "What good times we will have together," she exclaimed. "I'll work harder than ever and I'll see that Mildred works, too. You'll be proud of us when we come home."

The Storm Breaks

HELEN WAS spending her second year at Cambridge School and Mildred was still a pupil there. Mr. Gilman, the principal, was happy to have the two girls in his school. Helen was known all over America and having her and her sister as pupils was good advertising.

Unfortunately complications were developing. One morning Miss Sullivan and Helen had a conference with Mr. Gilman. "I'm eager to talk with you," said Helen. "The assistant principal thinks I may be ready for college in three years instead of four. Isn't that wonderful?"

Mr. Gilman frowned. "Four years are required for a normal girl to prepare for college," he spelled to her.

Miss Sullivan was standing beside her pupil. She looked hurt at his words. "Helen is a normal girl," she argued. "There is just one difference. I am her eyes and ears."

Mr. Gilman did not answer. Often he and Miss Sullivan disagreed concerning Helen. He went on spelling into the girl's hand, "In my opinion, you should remain here for five years. By that time, you should be ready for the entrance examinations for Radcliffe."

Helen's face fell. "But, sir, my teachers say I am doing excellent work in German, Latin, English, and Greek and Roman history."

"But you are not doing well in physics, geometry, and algebra," Mr. Gilman reminded her. "You must understand them, too."

Helen frowned. "I don't like those subjects. They don't make sense to me."

"You must have them to pass your college entrance examinations," Mr. Gilman insisted. "Three years here are not enough. We can't let you take the examinations until you are ready. Besides, Miss Sullivan is working you too hard."

This statement startled Miss Sullivan, because she felt it was untrue. Even so, she kept quiet for the sake of Helen.

Her pupil showed no such control. She stamped her foot and looked angry. "Teacher never makes me do anything I don't want to do," she said coldly. "She makes learning an adventure, Mr. Gilman. I'd be just a stupid young lady if she hadn't come to my rescue a long time ago. She never drives me to work. For this reason I won't allow you to talk about her working me too hard. She is the most wonderful woman in the whole world."

By now the girl was trembling from head to foot. Miss Sullivan took her arm and said, "Come

166

with me, Helen. Everything will be all right." The shaking girl allowed herself to be led away.

Mr. Gilman watched them leave with a glum look on his face. "Just as I said," he muttered. "That Miss Sullivan is a slave driver. Helen must remain here for five years. I shall not allow her to go a moment sooner."

During the next ten days Helen and Miss Sullivan kept out of Mr. Gilman's way. They attended classes as usual. They studied at night to prepare lessons for the next day. Matters seemed to cool down, but Miss Sullivan had an uneasy feeling something still might happen.

The days went on. In the meantime Mr. Gilman wrote secretly to Mrs. Keller in Alabama. Then one morning he called Helen and Miss Sullivan to his office, waving a telegram in the air.

"This should stop you," he said, reading the telegram to Miss Sullivan. " 'You are authorized to act as Helen's guardian. Kate A. Keller.' "

Miss Sullivan could hardly believe what she heard. She was sure there was a misunderstanding. There had always been love and respect between her and Mrs. Keller. Mr. Gilman had spelled the telegram into Helen's hand.

He turned once more to Miss Sullivan and said, "From now on I will conduct Helen's affairs. As long as you remain here with her, you will take orders from me."

Helen began to cry and felt for Teacher's hand, which was as cold as ice. Miss Sullivan tightened her grip on Helen's hand.

"Mr. Gilman, I can no longer remain at your school," she said. "I shall leave for Alabama at once and take Helen and Mildred with me. I am sure I can explain everything to Mrs. Keller, when I see her."

He gave a short laugh. "You may go as soon as you like. The girls will remain here. You forget that I am Helen's guardian."

A few hours later Helen and Mildred were in their bedroom. Miss Sullivan was busy packing her suitcase, getting ready to leave. Finally she put on her hat and went to face the cold December weather. She was upset but tried hard not to let the girls know how she felt.

"Be brave, my darlings," she begged them. "Everything will be all right with you."

Helen sobbed. "How could Mr. Gilman be so cruel?" she asked. "You have always been good and have thought of me first."

Miss Sullivan kissed her good-by. Then she kissed Mildred. "I am going to our friends, the Fullers," she told them. "I intend to fight back. I shall send a telegram to your mother. Dr. Bell will help us. So will Mr. Chamberlin in Wrentham. We are not alone."

After Miss Sullivan left, Helen threw herself across the bed and cried. Mildred sat on the bed and sobbed, too. The two girls felt that without Teacher nearby in the school, the bottom had dropped out of their world.

Before long Mr. Gilman came to the door to talk with the girls. He seemed to be very uneasy and cleared his throat before he began to speak. "You girls will come home with me," he said. "Then Mrs. Gilman will take care of you, until we make other arrangements."

Mildred spelled Mr. Gilman's words into Helen's hand. Then Helen sat up and said, "We will not come to your house, but we will stay right here until Teacher comes back. We do not like you, and we do not trust you."

The principal looked startled. Was this the gentle sixteen-year-old that he had said was overworked? She had plenty of fire and spirit today. He turned and walked away.

That night the two sisters cried themselves to sleep in each other's arms. Neither girl went to classes the next morning and nobody came near them. The hours passed slowly and quietly. At last Mildred heard footsteps in the hall coming toward their room. She rushed to open the door and cried, "Teacher, come in."

A glad smile went over Helen's face. She knew that Miss Sullivan had come back even before Mildred told her. They had a happy reunion in the center of the room. The fears of the night before were entirely swept away.

"Don't worry," said Miss Sullivan. "They must drag me out before I leave you again."

Mr. Chamberlin came at noon. He had been the first to receive a message from Miss Sullivan. Helen knew that their troubles were over when she felt the strong clasp of his hand. She knew that he could be trusted. "I have already talked with Mr. Gilman," he said. "Now all three of you are coming to Red Farm with me."

Three sighs of relief went up from three grateful people. They felt they could not stay at the

Cambridge School another minute. Mr. Chamberlin was like a hero who had come to deliver them from a dragon. Soon they were at Red Farm with the Chamberlin family. Already the recent events seemed like an unhappy dream.

The next day Mrs. Keller arrived. She was greatly disturbed and had taken a train as soon as she received Miss Sullivan's telegram. She sat on the sofa with her arms around her daughters and wanted to know what had happened.

After she was informed, she smiled at Miss Sullivan and said, "I was wrong in asking Mr. Gilman to act as Helen's guardian. He wrote me a most convincing letter. When he told me Helen's health was in danger, I lost my head. Please forgive me, Teacher."

"There is nothing to forgive," said Miss Sullivan. "You just didn't understand."

"I will never separate you from Helen again," Mrs. Keller declared. "Now we must decide

173

what to do. Of course she and Mildred cannot return to Mr. Gilman's school. That is out of the question. We must think of something else."

"We hope that Helen and Miss Sullivan will remain with us," said Mr. Chamberlin. "We will get a tutor from Harvard to help them."

"Now I'll have two more daughters in the house," said Mrs. Chamberlin gayly. "Miss Sullivan is so young and pretty that she could easily pass for Helen's sister."

Mrs. Keller decided to take Mildred home with her to Alabama. "Surely now our troubles are over," she said serenely. "According to the old saying, 'All's well that ends well.' "

College
and Beyond

THE CHAMBERLINS were as good as their word.
Helen and Miss Sullivan lived at Red Farm for
eight months. During the winter they spent
many happy hours tobogganing on the hillsides.
During the summer they hiked, rode horseback,
and went bicycling. Helen even learned to ride
a tandem, or bicycle built for two.

Even though there was time for playing, most
of Helen's time was devoted to work. Aunt
Eleanor Hutton had arranged for her to have a
tutor, named Merton S. Keith, from Harvard.
She wanted to learn as much as she could.

The following fall, Helen and Miss Sullivan

decided to return to Boston where Mr. Keith could tutor her more readily. She learned so fast that both Mr. Keith and Miss Sullivan had to work hard to keep up with her. Her friends thought that she never had looked healthier.

In June, 1899, Helen took her entrance examinations at Radcliffe and passed them with flying colors. She even won honors in advanced Latin. Now she was qualified for college, but the head of the school advised her to wait a year before entering. Accordingly, she studied one year more with Mr. Keith and enrolled at Radcliffe in the fall of 1900.

Both Helen and Miss Sullivan were happy at Radcliffe. They rented a house in Cambridge where friends constantly came to see them. Together they worked harder than they had ever worked, studying lessons and carrying on college activities. Without Teacher, it would have been impossible for Helen to succeed so well. She spelled constantly into Helen's hand and checked to make certain that Helen understood. Every night she went to bed exhausted.

When Helen was halfway through college, she was asked by Edward A. Bok, the editor of *Ladies Home Journal*, to write her life story for his magazine. Before accepting, she talked the matter over with Teacher, because she knew that much of the work would fall on her.

"It will be good to earn some money," said Helen. "We have money for my college education, but we'll need money after I graduate. Do you think I can write a book?"

"Yes, and Mr. Bok thinks you can," replied Miss Sullivan. "Your professor says you can write better than any pupil he has ever had."

So the book was begun. Helen called it *The Story of My Life*. Parts of it were to appear monthly in the *Ladies' Home Journal* before it was to be published in book form.

At first all went well. Helen enjoyed the excitement of being an author and found writing a pleasure. Soon, however, she found the load too heavy and began to fall behind in her classes. Night after night she lay awake and worried.

"It's well Mr. Gilman can't see you now," said Miss Sullivan. "Once more he would say that I am working you too hard."

"You are not to blame, Teacher," said Helen. "I simply need literary help."

Help came by way of a tall, handsome young man, named John Macy, from Harvard. He took time from teaching his English classes to help Helen with her story. With his help, she was able to meet each monthly deadline.

The *Story of My Life* came out as a book on March 21, 1903. Helen was overjoyed. Most of the reviews were excellent. Mark Twain wrote her, "I am charmed and enchanted with your book. You are a wonderful creature, the most wonderful in the world—you and your other half together—Miss Sullivan."

"I'm glad he mentioned you, Teacher," said Helen. "You deserve most of the credit."

Miss Sullivan gave her a friendly pat. "No, you provided the mind and I provided only the eyes and ears."

"Nothing of the sort," replied Helen. "You taught me to think. You taught me to enjoy books. You taught me to live."

"Maybe I helped," said Miss Sullivan lightly. "At least I hope so."

In June, 1904, Helen graduated *cum laude* (with honors) from Radcliffe. She was one of ninety-six girls. Teacher sat on the platform beside her and spelled into her hand. No one paid any attention to Miss Sullivan, but without her Helen could not have been there.

In the meantime Helen and Teacher had purchased an old farmhouse with seven acres of ground near Wrentham, Massachusetts. They went there after Helen graduated from Radcliffe. When Helen burst into the house, she exclaimed. "Now we can really enjoy life."

The house was located in a beautiful spot, with trees about and a lake nearby. There was room for horses, dogs, and other kinds of animals. Helen loved every inch of the place.

Soon their friends began to come to the old house. John Macy, who had helped Helen with her book, came oftener than others. Helen noticed how often he came, and said, "Teacher, I believe John likes to come here to see you."

Everything remained quiet and Helen understood. She was very happy to know that love had come at last to her beloved teacher. Finally Miss Sullivan came near and took her hand. "Yes, I'm in love, but I will never leave you," she said. "You can always count on me."

In May, 1905, John Macy and Anne Sullivan

180

were married in the sitting room of the old farm-house. It was a joyful day. Helen stood beside Miss Sullivan as the preacher performed the ceremony. She knew she was gaining a brother. John himself told her so.

After the wedding Helen went home to Alabama with her mother for a while. After a few weeks the Macys came back from their honeymoon. Then she returned to Wrentham to live with them.

For eight years Helen and the Macys lived happily in the old farmhouse. Helen and John wrote and Teacher kept house. They had many good friends who came and went. Everything seemed perfect.

Then little by little their happiness began to fade. In 1913 Helen went on a cross-country lecture tour accompanied by Teacher. She was starting a career of traveling, speaking, and writing that lasted the rest of her life.

All went well for a time, but Teacher's health was poor, and it soon became evident that she wouldn't be able to work as hard as she had before. Of course, Helen couldn't carry on without her. They discussed the matter at length and wondered what to do.

Finally they met a young woman from Scotland by the name of Polly Thompson. She wanted to work in America, and agreed to travel with them to relieve Teacher of many responsibilities. She bought train tickets, secured hotel rooms, ordered meals, and did a thousand and one things that Teacher had done before.

In the succeeding years Teacher's health became worse and she had to give up traveling completely. Finally in 1936 she died and Helen lost the dearest and most helpful friend she had ever had in life.

Lady with a Title

THE MEN in the long hospital ward were waiting for a visitor. They would not see her, for they were blind. She would not see or hear them, for she was Helen Keller.

A car stopped in front of the hospital. Presently the men in the beds heard footsteps in the hall. Several persons entered the far door. Then Nurse Margaret spoke. The men smiled a little. She was their favorite nurse.

"Here is the lady you have been waiting for," she told them. "Miss Keller has come to see you, just as she promised."

Every man turned eagerly toward the sound

of Nurse Margaret's voice. All of them wished they could see the great Miss Keller for they had heard many interesting things about her.

For a moment there was silence. Then a voice broke the stillness. It did not rise and fall as voices usually do, but its tone remained the same. It sounded somewhat like a machine. In a way it was a machine.

Helen Keller hadn't heard anyone speak since she was less than two years old. She had learned to speak without being able to hear other people speak. This had been difficult, but she hadn't given up until she learned.

"I am glad to be with you today, my friends," she said. "I appreciate your invitation to visit you. It is good to be wanted. I feel honored that you want me."

"Her voice certainly sounds strange," said a young man with bandages over his eyes.

"Be quiet," said the man next to him. "Only

a great person could have overcome the stumbling blocks she has met."

"I only meant that her voice is different," said the first man.

Helen Keller was still speaking. The sightless men listened to every word. Nurse Margaret never took her eyes off her. She could hardly realize that the tall, stylishly-dressed, friendly lady was Helen Keller herself.

"She seems so alive," the nurse whispered to Miss Thompson, who still was Miss Keller's traveling companion. By now she was almost as well known as Anne Sullivan had been before.

Miss Thompson laughed softly. She spoke with a slight Scots burr. "She's about the alivest person I know."

Both women turned toward Helen Keller. She was standing in the center of the room, with her hands tightly clasped. A smile lighted up her face as she spoke.

"I wish I could stay with you and really get to know you," she was saying, "but that is impossible. I am no longer young and have much to do. I travel far and wide for the American Foundation for the Blind. We must raise money to help persons who cannot see.

"We cannot stop with America. Workers for the blind all over the world have asked me to visit their countries. After my beloved teacher, Anne Sullivan Macy, died, I went with Polly Thompson on a 40,000-mile trip. We traveled to the ends of the earth and back."

The men lay in their beds and listened. As their visitor spoke, they no longer felt like prisoners because of their blindness. She was blind, and her blindness had not kept her from leading a full life.

Now through Helen Keller's words, they shook hands with Winston Churchill in England. They paused briefly in the shrine of Mahatma

Gandhi in India. They petted a friendly koala bear in Australia. They felt a sheaf of wheat in Israel. They smelled sweet flowers in Hawaii.

"This was not a pleasure trip," she reminded them. "I went to see for myself the blind of other countries. I found that you and I are not alone, but that blindness is a world problem. There are others like us everywhere. There are hands stretched out to help us. We must in turn stretch out our hands to help others."

A small sigh went up here and there. The men wondered whether they really could learn to help others. She certainly was helping them now, yet she could neither see nor hear.

"We have our work to do," Helen Keller told them. "I do not know why I am blind. I do not know why you are. Yet I am sure that God has a real purpose for us all. It is our business to find out what that purpose is."

Before Helen Keller left, she stopped at every

188

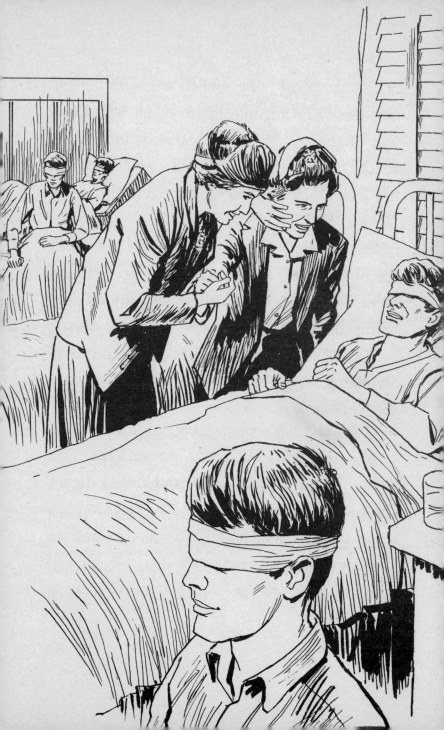

bed in the ward. She spelled out with her fingers greetings into the hands of all who knew sign language. She gave warm handclasps to all the others. Everywhere it seemed as if a fresh breeze were sweeping through the ward.

Soon the lights would be turned off for the night. Somehow there was a different air about the place. The men seemed hopeful. Some of them even laughed and joked. Nurse Margaret hummed a tune as she passed from bed to bed.

"You sound as happy as Miss Keller did," said a young man. "I can't explain it, but she made me feel happy, too."

Nurse Margaret plumped up the young man's pillows. "Isn't that wonderful?" she said.

"Yes, it is," he answered slowly. "She didn't seem to feel particularly sorry for us. She just made us realize that we have work to do."

The nurse almost held her breath. She could hardly believe her ears. This patient had been one of the gloomiest of all. Sometimes he had wished aloud that he wouldn't have to go on living. Now he raised himself on one elbow and gave his pillows a good, healthy thump.

"I'm getting out of here as fast as I can," he declared. "Already I've stayed here too long. Now I'm confident that I can find a way to make a living. Miss Keller said that I can."

Nurse Margaret nodded. "There are many ways a blind person can make a living," she said. "We have workers here in the hospital who will be glad to help you find a good way."

"I'll see them tomorrow." He laughed aloud at the idea of using the word *see*. "That's the way Miss Keller talks. I guess there's more than one way of seeing."

Nurse Margaret gave him a friendly pat. "Good boy!" she said.

He smiled up at her. "I'm grateful to you and all the other nurses and the doctors for what you have done for me here. You have been good to me. But Miss Keller reminded me that I am a man and have a man's work to do. What a remarkable woman she is."

"Yes, what a remarkable woman!" echoed Nurse Margaret. "Pehaps that is why she has a title such as she has."

"I didn't know that she had a title," said the young man in surprise. "I thought that only former royal persons had titles. I thought that titles had gone out of style."

"Not her kind," the nurse told him. "Her title is 'America's First Lady of Courage.'"

The young man lay back on his pillows with a grin on his face. He looked sure of himself as if he was ready to get up and be on his way. "Let's not be selfish about her," he said. "I have a better title for her. My title for her is 'The World's First Lady of Courage.'"